# LADY IN THE BAY

By

## M. A. Cole

**LADY IN THE BAY**

**ISBN**: 979-8-218-02997-5

# To My Greatest Treasure

# TABLE OF CONTENTS

# CIGAR STORE INDIAN

**Y**ou definitely can't tell a kid a story about someone that a Disney movie was based on and not expect them to be anything other than overly excited after hearing it. For me and my best friend, Claire, even from a very early age, we were more than just a little intrigued. That ever-growing curiosity may have started the first time an old man named Ikey P. Rolfe told us about who he called, "the lady in the bay," but we were just as consumed with all of the twists and turns that old man seemed to purposefully add to his tale over the years. Looking back at his perpetual embellishments, they all seemed to be so strategically placed, and when it came to Claire and I they always seemed to contain just the right amount of encouragement to set us out on our own youthful adventures. When I think about that old man and how he so proudly passed his hidden lessons on to his young followers, I honestly believe they achieved everything that he intended them to. Ikey was definitely unlike anyone that I had ever met.

I never knew how old he was, but to us kids, he looked ancient, really-really Wooly Mammoth, or even Mastodon ancient. Ikey was a tall, slender man and he had the darkest brown wrinkled skin. It was almost as if he was forever etched and tinted from obviously rarely ever leaving the direct blast of the sun. He also had this majestic semi-long, flowing white hair that seemed to glow as a full moon would, that is if he ever took his hat off long enough for anyone to actually get a peek at it. I knew he had his own house somewhere but I don't think he ever went to it because, no matter whether it was early in the morning or very late at night, he always seemed to be outside doing something. Most of the time, whatever that something was, had to do with helping my grandfather in some way or being near that saltwater that was so graciously wrapped all around the tiny island that we were on. To say the least, Ikey was a very unique man. He always seemed to touch everyone's life in just the right way, and most often, his touch occurred when his intended recipients needed it the most.

The funny thing is, regardless of his leathered outward appearance, he had these deep, dark, crystal blue eyes and a supremely kind and protective heart that seemed to be as youthful as anyone's ever was. If your eyes are truly the windows to the soul, Ikey's were so pure that you could almost see all the way to the bottom of his essence. It was always a welcomed and profoundly regal sight too. My family's friendship with Ikey would last many lifetimes, although they rarely outlasted his. He proudly gave credit for his longevity to claims of being a descendant of a great Powhatan Indian Chief. I don't know if he was an actual Native American kind of Indian or not, but he certainly did look the part and he spoke it just as well. The one thing I know for a fact was if Ikey had something to say, there was definitely going to be a few strategically placed enhancements along the way but also a surprising amount of hidden truths to his words as well. Ikey's stories may not have revealed themselves in the exact way he told them, but there was always a lesson to be learned and a mission to be off on after hearing such possibilities.

Speaking of real-life Indian's, the first time I met Ikey was outside of an old country store, a little store on Gwynn's Island named Scrooch's. My grandfather chewed tobacco, and one afternoon, much to his chagrin, he completely ran out of his greatly treasured commodity. In response to his dilemma, we had to make an emergency trip to that quaint little store. The rest, for my family anyway, was history. The first day I met Ikey, long before I knew what a cigar store Indian was, I thought I was seeing one. He was leaning on the corner of that old building with his hat perched down over his face, and he—or what I thought was an, "it"— wasn't moving a muscle. I honestly couldn't tell if the man was real or not at that time. As my grandfather and I got out of the truck to enter the store, that old man who I very much thought was a wooden statue still didn't move, not even after I accidentally brushed up against him as we passed by.

After my grandfather bought plenty chewing tobacco, he started to head out the door. He then turned and yelled back at me to hurry up because, as usual, I was stuck in this one particular aisle looking at the candy bars and lagging behind. As I promptly followed my grandfather's directions, I thought to myself, most of that building had these huge bay windows across the front, so I would have thought that I would have seen someone steal that wooden Indian from in front of the store after we came in, but I didn't. I looked all around, and he or it, wasn't anywhere to be seen. I wasn't brave enough to say anything to my grandfather because I didn't want him to think I was going completely nuts from seeing things that weren't actually there. So, as I had to do many times in my youth, I just marked my sighting and its disappearance up to my imagination. When I got in the truck, however, my imagination and the rest of me almost jumped through the roof of that old truck because that cigar store Indian that was just so motionlessly leaning against that old brick building was now in the truck with us.

At first, all my youthful mind could come up with was that my grandfather must have stolen the thing, but, before it could register with me that would never happen, I fully realized the man who was now right directly beside me was very real after all. I'm sure, based on my facial expression, my grandfather and the man who would later introduce himself as Ikey P. Rolfe had to know what I was thinking but I still wouldn't dare ever admit to it. After Ikey introduced himself, he asked for a ride to wherever it was we were going. I thought to myself, *well, since I'm going nuts, you can come too*, but then I remembered it wasn't really my decision to make. My grandfather was still laughing at me and the overly surprised look that I guess I still had on my face. Laughing or not though, he didn't seem to mind taking a complete stranger back to the house with us. I guess, for some unknown reason, my grandfather trusted Ikey from the very first time he met him. I know my family has been very grateful he did ever since.

From that first day, there were very few other days that Ikey wasn't either helping my grandfather with something or playing and telling stories with the kids of my family. There were times where he'd just seemed to be hanging out looking over us though. I would think it would almost be like the royal guard does in front of Buckingham Palace, but our royal guard just happened to be really-really tan and really-really old too. I believe originally, I just thought we adopted an old, brown man but, later, I clearly knew it was definitely the other way around most of the time. In a very short amount of time, Ikey became as much of a part of our family as any of the rest of us were. It was a strange way to become related, but with Ikey, the stranger things seemed to be, the more they'd somehow end up helping those who wouldn't have let it happen any other way.

My grandfather wasn't an overly young man himself when we first met Ikey but he still had to be ten or more years younger than Ikey was if I had to guess. I think the way my grandfather saw Ikey that first day in front of Scrooch's little country store could define him as well as anything could. My grandfather believed in people and the possible greatness of everyone, regardless of what they looked like or where they came from. In this case, evidentially, it didn't matter to him what store they motionlessly stood in front of either. With him, success wasn't about how big your achievements were. In his way of thinking and how he often explained it to us, his family, true success in life was more about how well you made the effort to care of others. He also told us that life rarely ever works out the way that anyone plans but you just can't ever stop trying or stubbling forward, as he's say. Somehow, without moving an inch that day, Ikey more than fit into my grandfather's defining insights, and, in doing so, he was as right about a person as he'd ever been. My grandfather came from extremely modest beginnings.

His start in life was pretty much like what most American's experienced throughout the great depression; it was a struggle from the start.  He was proud that he had to work so hard for everything he had though. Life for him and many others back then wasn't easy but, in his case, he always made it his prime mission to provide the things for his family that he was rarely afforded in his own youth. His most passed along lesson and one he said he learned very early in life was, "If you didn't work, you didn't eat," and that big man liked to eat a lot, so he worked a lot too. His ambition and love for his family helped him not only work his way out of extreme poverty, it also took him to a place that even he never thought he'd end up: a tiny island near the mouth of the Chesapeake Bay and Piankatank River. That little place, he soon found out, was named Gwynn's Island. I once asked him how he found such a tiny place in the middle of the water next to nowhere.

He sarcastically responded as he often did, "With my truck." He then laughed and told me the irony of his bad joke wasn't very far from the actual truth. One day, he and one of his older brothers just went for a drive and somehow they ended up there after they ran out of road. Most of my relatives were originally from Rosehill, North Carolina and they were poor, especially my grandfather's side of the family. He said the only clothes he wore for many years were made from used burlap feed sacks. Being a little spoiled and from the suburbs, I'd never worn anything made from a burlap sack before so all I could think about was how itchy that must have been. He told us that his standard attire never changed until he joined the military. That's where they finally issued him real clothes, as he called them. He was extremely proud of his military days too and the start in life that he let everyone know the military provided for our family. I know his "real clothes" recollection very well because his hardheaded grandson—me—was often re-told that story whenever I wanted something that he thought may not have been as needed as I believed it was.

If Ikey was tall, my grandfather was taller, and a lot bigger around too. I think he was what most people would consider as huge. He had the biggest hands of any human I've ever seen, and his powerful fingers looked more like sausage rolls than anything else I can think of to compare them to. He was uncommonly strong too. I've seen him lean over and snatch car engines out completely by himself and those giant paws of his on more than one occasion. He had to work so hard in his youth that, similar to Ikey, he could do just about anything that ever needed to be done. He'd soon learn that, with his new island venture, there were always plenty of things that needed his attention too. The main difference between Ikey and my grandfather when it came to work was, although my grandfather could eventually fix anything, he'd always seem to break it worse than it originally was before it actually got better.

My grandfather's multiple attempts at a job, or his "little projects" as he called them, often drove Ikey nuts but my grandfather never seemed to care. He always enjoyed Ikey's company, so he'd just keep fixing, breaking and then fixing again whatever it was he was working on. For me, I think I only paid attention to the breaking things part of my grandfather's and Ikey's lessons because I'm still not very handy like those two old men were. I really liked the times when Ikey would fuss at my grandfather though. I secretly felt like I was getting in a little unrevealed redemption in but, once again, I'd never admit to it. Most of the time, Ikey's comical recommendations were more supportive than they were anything else though. He called my grandfather Billy, and I heard him say at least a thousand times in my life, "Billy, now you know that doesn't go there," or "Billy, you should do this first, don't you think?" The two men sounded like a bunch of old hens bantering back and forth, but I know each of them was helping the other in ways that big, tough, old men would never admit to.

I could tell my grandfather truly appreciated his older friend's guidance, especially if it saved him a few dollars, but it was still good to see the shoe on the other foot at times. Another difference between my grandfather and Ikey was, my grandfather would work all day and half the night, if not more, on most days. Ikey, on the other hand, couldn't or at least wouldn't. Ikey would take breaks to go fishing, take walks, or really go and do anything else he wanted to do other than work. His life included work but it wasn't all about work as my grandfather's seemed to be most of the time. On many of Ikey's planned hiatuses, he'd come over and play with us kids. I'm pretty sure that's also when his self-declared professional storytelling career began also. At first, it was just me and Claire, but later, another friend, Jonas, would sit down with us on a little beach near the bay for what seemed like hours listening to every single word that kind, old tanned man had to say.

My grandfather built himself up to the point that, after the military, he was eventually able to buy a small restaurant in Richmond, where I was born. Even though his last name was Hanchey, he still couldn't afford to spell out his whole last name on his first storefront sign, so he named that little place, Hank's; Hank's BBQ to be exact. It was about two hours away from Gwynn's Island and, just like compound interest, all of his early work efforts multiplied and paid off to the point where he was able to set out to look for a new financial opportunity, and of course, more work. Why he chose to build a campground, no one ever knew, but that's exactly what he decided his new venture should be. He built Camper's Haven on the tip of that small Island in the late sixties. He didn't do it alone though. Almost all of our family and many of his friends helped in one way or another, especially my grandmother. She worked every bit as hard as he did, she just did it in different ways. My grandmother was the unquestionable and undisputed heart of our family and she more than had his heart too.

Even though it didn't always seem like it, we all knew that almost everything he ever did was for her in his own way. He wanted her and all of his family to be as far away from the struggles of his youth as possible, so, simply put, he worked his way away from them. Even though he did finally gain a little financial freedom, he never gave up his survivalist mentality. He always felt and often let us know that if somebody else could do something, so could he. The "he" in this story often meant, 'so could we', but whether it was putting in a pier, clearing a field, or really anything in between. We did that and so many other somewhat creative things over the two years it took to make that raw island land into a campground. Usually, when people are professionals at what they do, they have all the proper equipment needed for the job. Don't get me wrong, the job always got done, and it was always a great finished product, but my grandfather always seemed to improvise much more than anyone probably ever should. I guess you'd call that diligence or even efficiency, but the truth of the matter was, sometimes, it was just plain dangerous.

Jokingly, but not so jokingly, the first time I ever questioned if that man really loved me or not was when we were putting in our first pier on the campground. I don't know about now, but back then, we used this huge water jet machine. It looked somewhat like a bazooka and it was every bit as big as I was, if not bigger. If you wanted a hole dug somewhere, you'd basically stick the end of that thing where you wanted it and then pray a little bit while holding on to it as tight as you could. From there, it did all the work blasting all of the sand and mud out of the way. The problem was the only machine we had to do that with back then was totally powered by electricity. If there was ever a time for a tool to be gas-powered, I would think when you're setting poles for a pier in the middle of the water would be it. That big man had me hold this massive power cord with raw wire poking out and half wrapped in electrical tape over my head in an aluminum johnboat.

To make matters worse, water would splash up in that little aluminum boat from every direction from him pulling it around by a rope to wherever it was that he wanted another hole pumped out. I wasn't allowed to cuss back then but I'm sure even then I was thinking, *Damn, what the hell, man!* If that was it, I'd say maybe he just had a momentary lapse in judgment about my actual safety, but it wasn't. It wasn't even close to being the last time some crazy mess like that happened. Those were the few times that Ikey wasn't anywhere to be found. I knew Ikey was smarter than the rest of us, and there had to be a reason for his life expectancy to still be greater than ours. Ikey proved both of those thoughts by disappearing when he felt someone actually had a chance of dying during our so-called little project times. The more my grandfather used the words "little project," the more dangerous I think everyone knew the job would be and the further away Ikey seemed to be away from it. One of many things I did love about back then was my grandfather had a lot of heavy equipment around during the construction years.

He had an old dump truck, an even older bulldozer, and one of the oldest tractors still in use in North America. He got them all working perfectly but just like Ikey they still had some substantial age on them. He also had an old, rusty road grader that almost looked like a giant brontosaurus chewing up the land as it came through. Evidentially those types of vehicles didn't require a license because I was the one who he often told to jump on and push over this tree or that pile of stumps. He was never too far away, but he certainly never seemed to appreciate my age, or lack thereof, either. I have to admit, I did feel like a king on those giant machines and, after a long day of doing whatever it was he told me to do, my chest seemed to be a little more pumped up than on most days. On the most special days, we'd even ride on those big machines together and I don't think many other things made him much prouder.

He was a good man, and watching him work so hard every single day of his life for what I knew was his way of providing for his family still gives me a great respect for him, in fact, a respect like no other. I do feel that he missed out on many of the things that his own hands built, but, for him, if it was for his family, then he was content enough with just being able to do it for us. When Ikey saw the super dangerous little projects calm down a bit, he'd show back up. I'm sure even he figured not too much could happen on the day he decided to go with my grandfather on what would seem like a routine trip to the landfill. That old dump truck that they jumped in was always overloaded with stumps and brush and things of that nature. This time, it was as packed down as much as it ever was. After Ikey got inside the cab of the truck, my grandfather started to pull off. As soon as he did, the dump bed immediately slammed open and dug itself into the ground. I think it wanted to prove to my grandfather that he, evidently, forgot to latch the dump bed.

This digging in the ground caused the whole dump truck to stretch out in the air more vertically than any old dump truck ever should. As it pointed straight up to the sky, it looked exactly like a rocket ship preparing to launch. Both of those old men were probably holding on to everything they could for their very unexpected journey upward. My grandmother and I watched it all happen from the front porch. At first, we were scared for them, but after a few seconds, we heard my grandfather fussing and mostly cussing about his dump truck's new positioning. Once we knew everything was more or less okay, we couldn't help but laugh out loud at what we had front row seats to see. Neither one of us would have ever thought a dump truck could ever do anything like that, but it did and when it did my grandfather kept yelling out, "My damn tobacco!" "My damn tobacco!"

As he kept repeating himself, my grandmother and I kept laughing harder and harder because we could only imagine what the inside of that dump truck looked like after that trip. He always had spit cups laying around, as he called them. The particular spit cup that he had with him in the dump truck that day obviously didn't like the unexpected ride and, in an act of defiance, decided to spill all over the place. Watching those two old men climb down from that erect dump truck would have been funny enough, but when Ikey made his way to the front porch, neither my grandmother nor myself had any chance of catching our breath anytime soon. Ikey was absolutely covered from head to toe in that nasty tobacco juice. Somehow it missed my great, big grandfather all together, but again, it didn't seem to miss any part of Ikey's poor, old, brown body. I don't think Ikey knew whether to throw up or punch my grandfather in the nose but, either way, once the men finally scaled their way down, Ikey huffingly made his way over to the porch to go inside and clean that slimy mess off of him.

This time, Ikey was the one saying, "That damn tobacco," and what made things even funnier—if that was possible—was, being that my grandfather was so much bigger than Ikey, Ikey had no other choice but to put on some of my grandmother's clothes until his were all washed up. I still couldn't breathe from laughing so hard, but after Ikey came back outside, I thought my insides were going to bust. There he was, a six-foot-tall, extremely tanned old man wearing four feet of clothes. His borrowed apparel wasn't what you'd call long pants, and they weren't shorts on him either. They looked more like culottes and, to make matters worse for him, they were pink ones at that. Looking back at our time at the campground, there were so many of those kinds of stories. I honestly don't know how any of us ever made it through them alive, even our super precautious royal guardsman, but we did.

The only real negative that ever came out of that particular time was that Ikey definitely would never ride in a dump truck with my grandfather again. If my grandfather would ask, Ikey would just shake his head and say, "That damn tobacco." I don't think my grandfather realized how much work a campground would be after it opened. I believe he thought that he put so much time and money into getting it ready that, once it opened, all he would have to do was just a little maintenance here or there. Once again, he couldn't have been any more wrong. We had everything that anyone would ever need or want for that matter, to include the wonderful Chesapeake Bay within walking distance, but we also had more than plenty to do, which often prevented us from taking that walk. The good thing was, although the camperly duties never seemed to end, at least at first, we always did what we needed to do together. Ikey was there most of the time too, provided it didn't have anything to do with that old dump truck or anything else that he thought may have an excessive amount of danger attached to it.

One of my grandfather's first rather unique challenges as a new campground owner was to get rid of some pests. These pests flew through the air and drew blood when they landed on your skin. In his efforts to hunt down all those ever-biting, pesky mosquitoes, he bought a huge bug killing thingamajig that he pulled behind the tractor. It was basically two fifty-gallon barrels mounted in the middle of a trailer with a lawnmower engine on one side and a long fire hose attached to the other. I can remember originally thinking how cool that thing was until we actually had to use it. This was definitely the second time that I jokingly, yet, not so jokingly, asked myself if my grandfather really loved me or not. Everything about that monstrous machine would be illegal as hell today but, without a doubt, I'm sure it was back then as well. Regardless of its status with the law, we did as we always did back then and improvised to press on with that particular little project.

Before we started my grandfather had me load some kind of silty jet-black powder in those big barrels. I guess since we were loading death into the machine, it at least had to look like death, and it did too. As I tried to pour that obviously, "hazardous to your health" mixture into the first tank, an equally black powdery cloud unexpectedly blew back up in my face. I gagged and coughed and most likely looked like Oliver Twist with a face full of soot after he popped out of one of those chimneys. This was my grandfather's and Ikey's turn to laugh pretty heavily at my expense. Once their unappreciated chuckles lessened, they finally got the engine of that stupid contraption running. Ikey quickly noticed that whatever it was supposed to be doing, it wasn't. Per the orders from his elderly advisor, my grandfather started tugging on the nozzle that was on the end of the hose. He kept opening and closing it in efforts to try and make something deadly happen. It didn't take too many yanks on that hose until something equally amusing to me set in as payback. We now had Oliver Twist and his grandfather covered in soot and Ikey was rolling.

Ikey laughed so hard that, as he doubled over trying to catch his breath, his false teeth fell half way out of his mouth. Even if we didn't know what we were doing most of the time with our little projects, they usually had quite a humorous surprise spring out somewhere along the way. This little toxic project was undoubtedly no different. Once the theatrics slowed down a bit, we finally got that machine working as they thought it should. At first, it started out by puffing out these little, black clouds one by one—the *I think I can, I think I can* type—then the clouds multiplied many times over, making everything around us as pitch black as the silty stuff we put into the machine in the first place. Eventually, those clouds got so black that my grandfather actually pulled out a flashlight in order for us to be able to finish the job. I later found out that concoction's name was dichlorodiphenyltrichloroethane, or DDT for short.

# CLAIRE'S LITTLE VOICE

**A**nything with a name that long or clouds that black needed to be as illegal as it was too. We all coughed up greyish phlegmy remnants of that stuff we breathed in for weeks, but afterward, our mosquito problem was gone and probably a good chunk of our future lung capacity along with it. I knew my grandfather didn't play when he had a job to do, regardless of the cost but, once again, I had to be thinking, *Damn, what the hell, man?* After the first few months of handling the craziest, most unexpected kinds of problems like the DDT delivery incident, the campground did start to run a little smoother. This finally allowed me, the kid, to be able to act like a kid a little more. I almost forgot that we were working most of the time though because of all of the absolutely ridiculously absurd things that always seemed to happen during our so-called little project time with my grandfather. Regardless of my original experiences, once I got a chance to actually get into that bay and really start acting my age, I soon remembered the difference. I'm glad I got to spend as much time as I did with my grandfather, but I definitely felt that my life was in danger many of those times too.

Usually, after dinner, my grandmother and I would go fishing for about an hour or so each evening. It was just as special as when my grandfather and I would ride on the bulldozer or road grader together. This was our time, and regardless whether we caught any fish or not, I always felt like I won a prize for her giving me so much of her time. If there was ever anyone that I could talk to about anything, it was my grandmother and I talked to her about everything too. I never really kept anything from her. Now, she had a very similar past as my grandfather, so she was pretty tough in her own right, if not even more. She, however, definitely had a much healthier and safer parental way about her. To prove how tough she was too I can remember one time when we were fishing, I got this huge jerk on my line.

I didn't know what was on the other end, but it bent my rod over so much that, when I stood up to reel whatever it was in, my feet started sliding towards the edge of the pier. My grandmother realized whatever it was wanted to catch me as much as I wanted to catch it. With her obviously remembering how much a new rod and reel cost and, similar to what my grandfather would have said, she made it very clear for me not to let go of that expensive rod. She then grabbed me around my waist in her efforts to slow down my expected future splash in the bay and to put a little extra insurance on my fishing rig, or so I thought? As I reeled and reeled for what seemed like half an hour, something I'd never seen before bobbed its head up over the waves, then it rippled itself back down underneath the water. This happened over and over again. Every time it would go back under, the slack in my line would screech back out and I'd have to, unfortunately, start reeling it in all over again. My arms were so tight and tired that they began to do a little more than hurt.

I knew that when dealing with either one of my grandparents, I better finish what I started, so I quietly kept reeling in whatever that thing was on the end of my line, pain and all. Once I finally got that monster closer to the pier, I saw that it was a giant, brown skate. It was so big that I guess some of the other aquatic life had mistaken it for a boat or something because it actually had barnacles attached to the underside of its giant wings. My rare catch made one last attempt at freedom. As it did, it headed back under the water for what I thought would be its last time. Instead of giving up and letting me catch the doggone thing, its last attempt at freedom broke my line. As I wiped the sweat of failure off of my forehead from something that wasn't supposed to feel like work, my grandmother gave out another one of those belly laughs. She laughed almost as hard as she did with Ikey and the dump truck tobacco juice incident. Then she started pointing down at the water to let me in on the joke.

As I looked to where she told me to, I saw that brown behemoth bobbing up and down with the waves, and I could swear every time it did, it stuck its tongue out at me. It was almost as if it was symbolically saying, "Not today, sucker." I didn't even know those stupid things had tongues. As our workdays usually ended, so did our nights of fishing, which was almost always in laughter about something crazy that always seemed to happen. I know I'll always cherish all the time that I got to spend with both of my grandparents. I can't call what my grandparents gave me as tough love because it was never tough, but it wasn't exactly normal all the time either. I guess I'll just call it odd—oddly beautiful love from some pretty terrific, loving, and beautifully odd people at times. As the campground became more like my grandfather had hoped, I was given more of my own time to reasonably roam. They knew I wasn't going to do anything too crazy because my grandfather would have probably made me dig a sewer line or something similar, so I guess that made me somewhat trustworthy.

One day, on one of my first solo adventures out, I saw a little girl who looked to be about the same age I was. She was playing in the sand and she evidentially had earned a little trust of her own because she was all by herself too. I confidently decided to go over and introduce myself. As I sat down beside her, I told her my name was Henry. If it wasn't her wavy, blonde hair or her cute, little, rosy cheeks, or even her own perfectly round, crystal-blue eyes, it was her voice. When that little girl said, "Hello" and told me her name was Claire, I was done. Instantly I fully realized that I'd never felt that way before and I had absolutely no idea why I was feeling that way then either. All at once, I seemed to learn how to stutter from out of nowhere too. All it took was hearing that little blonde girl's voice for the first time. My family had all boys and we were pretty rough around the edges. I guess that's where our well-learned survival tactic came from, but I'd never seen or definitely never heard anyone my age like Claire before, not even at school.

Once my ridiculous and unexpected nervousness wore off, I was actually able to complete full sentences again. From there, we talked on the beach and played in the sand for so long that day that it felt like we knew each other since the beginning of time, our limited time on earth anyway. Her family actually lived on the island and had for a long time. Claire and her parents had been playing on that little beach long before my grandfather ever thought about buying it or turning its surroundings into a campground. This, however, was the first time that I ever saw her, and I was sure glad that my adventures of that day produced who would soon become my best friend for life. As we were playing, Ikey walked up and, as old people sometimes do, he kind of creepily said, "Hey, what do we have here?" He then winked at both of us. Claire's plump, little cheeks became instantly even rosier than before and I tried to ignore my old tan friend by looking down at my lap hoping he'd go away. What was obvious to everyone was that Claire and I definitely liked each other from the very start and from that very first day, wherever one of us went, the other wasn't far behind.

It was that way from my very first stutter-infused introduction and it stayed that way for a long time. Surprisingly, or maybe not, my grandfather didn't care if Claire was a little girl or not because that overly industrious big man would also risk her life at times too. In a much more normal manner, my grandmother would often invite Claire to go fishing with us after dinner as well. I didn't think life could get much better than it was but with that little blonde girl, it did. We were just a couple of innocent kids planting some pretty remarkable seeds. For some reason, from that very first day, we both expected whatever it was that we were experiencing to last a lifetime. I guess, in other words, some people that come into your life just seem to fit, no matter what age you are or what you've ever been through. You just know they are as unexplainable as it is, a predestined gift from above. Claire was that for me and I always knew I was that for her too.

I guess because I started spending so much time with Claire and, thankfully, my grandfather seemed to have a handle on most of his so-called little projects, I think Ikey began to feel a little lonely and left out. I can't claim to have ever been a psychiatrist for the tanned elderly but I'm guessing he thought he needed to find a best friend of his own now too. Ikey, however, was from the old school, the old-old school and, in his playful way, he'd joked around with me about how I could learn a thing or two from the romance master. Well, this great and mighty romance master ended up stuttering even worse than I did the first time he met this nice lady named Miss Anna. In fairness, I guess smitten is smitten no matter what age you are. I knew Ikey's wife passed away long before we met him and, with the exception of my family, I could imagine he could get pretty lonely at times but the first day Ikey met who he was so smitten with, all I could do was shake my head. Romeo P. Rolfe, as I called him, actually dressed up in a suit that no one ever knew he had.

That was fine and he really did look kind of sharp, but the problem was, when he went to introduce himself to that nice lady at campsite seven, it was at least a hundred degrees outside. Since he asked me to be his sidekick for his first visit, I dressed appropriately. I wore shorts, a t-shirt and tennis shoes. Our walk there was only a short distance, but it was really-really hot. It was so hot that by the time Ikey knocked on the lady's front door he was drenched in sweat. When she opened the door and saw Ikey in such a moist state, she had to be thinking that something was terribly wrong with her unexpected and uninvited visitor. She quickly grabbed him by the arm and rushed him inside. What made it worse was how he was so comically flubbering his own words around this time. She was probably thinking, *why did this old, tan man come to my door just to have a stroke on the front steps?*

This lady was younger than Ikey but not by much and maybe just a little older than my grandfather, but once she realized what his true reasons were for being there, and after their own awkward introductory moments, they sounded just as giddy as I'm sure Claire and I did the first day we met. Miss Anna was really nice to us both, and she let us know right away that she was from Germany and she really enjoyed baking. I knew the campground was pretty nice by this point, but not nice enough to make that drive from Germany, I thought. She later told us that she retired several years ago and enjoyed her time at the Island so much on a prior visit that she decided to stay and live there year-round. Ikey eventually did dry off and straighten up as much as he could. When I could tell he was back to his old wise-ish self, I decided to head back home. Before I left, Miss Anna told me that I had to take some of her German treats that she just finished baking home with me.

I was like my grandfather; I liked to eat, so I graciously waited for her to pack a plate of something that I believe she called Fran Brotchen for my trip back home. All I know is, she told me they were these sweet, buttery cinnamon biscuit treats from her homeland and then strongly advised me to wait until I got home before I ate any. She said they'd most likely still be too hot to eat for a while. That nice baking lady may not have remembered how hot it was outside but Ikey and I sure did. I didn't know how much cooling off those things would do anyway because I knew, cool or not, there was no chance of those things making it all the way home. When I put that first bite of that Fanny Brotto—or whatever you call that sugary cinnamon biscuit treat—in my mouth, I think my teeth got jealous because I didn't even have to chew. That tasty German snack was even better than when you put cotton candy on your tongue and just let it melt away in all of its sugary magnificence. As I smacked my lips in my own version of culinary appreciation, I began to fully realize that the campground was really beginning to become quite a gathering place for some pretty colorful characters.

One of those highly colorful characters who often collected himself around the campground was a man named Conway. We called him, Conway the Crab Man because, well…duh…he was the local crab man. As brown as Ikey was, Conway was just as dark, but he was dark red. I don't know if it was because his skin didn't react quite the same way to the sun that Ikey's did or whether it was because of all those Coors Lights that had to be raising his blood pressure to a level that was somewhere out of sight. Either way, he glowed for an entirely different reason. Conway was a funny man too. It may have been because of all those silver bullets or maybe he really was as happy as he always seemed to be. He always kept everyone around him in stitches. About every other word that came out of his mouth was a curse word. When he'd realize that kids were around, as we often were, he'd smack his lips as if he were punishing his own mouth for letting those types of words out in the first place.

He also spoke with the local Gwynn's Island dialect that, to be truthful, I could hardly understand at times, especially if he was on his second or third six-pack. People like Conway made me see why my grandfather fit in so well on the Island. Even though Conway drank and cussed a lot, he also worked a lot himself too. He provided fresh crabs to all the local restaurants and to anyone else who wanted them. Regardless of any state of mind the blue mountains may have placed him in, he took great pride in throwing the crabs that needed to grow a little more back. He only wanted to give out the absolute best that beautiful bay had to provide, so that's what he always did. Conway was also the first person to call us, "Come-here's." At first, I didn't know exactly what a "Come-here" was, but after I thought about it a little bit, the name kind of spoke for itself. The locals, as Conway was, not only took great pride in their work but also in their surroundings.

I believe the nickname was more of a signal to people who weren't from the Island to make sure we appreciated it the same way they did. Many of the locals could trace their relatives back for generations, even back to colonial days and beyond. We understood our nickname but, to be truthful, I think once the locals realized that my grandfather was probably more like they were than they originally would expect him to be, they became as hospitable as anyone ever has ever been to my family. There was one sole exception, however—a teenager who worked at the post office on the island. His name was Tommy, and he didn't like anyone who wasn't from the island, so I stayed away from him for the most part. The little post office where he worked was so small it was often just him working and he let everyone know he had complete control over everyone's mail coming in and leaving the island. Going back to likes and dislikes, the only thing I didn't like was Conway's dog. The Crab Man had a three-legged, grey greyhound named Pogo. I guess when he named him, he sarcastically figured that dog would just be hopping around all the time.

I always thought that even I could outrun a three-legged dog, but I had no chance to ever get away from that grey greyhound. Those things are fast, no matter how many legs they have. What made things worse with Pogo was he never seemed to like me very much either. Looking back I think it was just Tommy and Pogo that I ever had any sort of cross thought about throughout my entire childhood on the island. Every time Pogo saw me, I honestly believed he just wanted to play, but he always ended up trying to hump my leg instead. In response to that dog's unwanted advances, I'd always try and push him off as fast as I could. Nine times out of ten our interactions ended up with him showing me his teeth and growling. Tommy may not have gone for the legs, but he also seemed to growl at me when he saw me too. On my way home that day, I had my last German Frankenstein—or whatever the name of that wonderful, sugary cinnamon biscuit treat was—in my pocket.

Then I noticed that dumb humpty-hump dog was on his way after me again. Miss Anna saved me and my leg that day though. Before Pogo could even get close enough to try and molest me once more, I threw my last sugary biscuit thing on the ground. It was a difficult thing to do because they were so delicious, but I knew it was for a good cause. That dog obviously thought those sugary cinnamon biscuit treats were as good as I did because he slurped it down in a hurry, then licked his lips like I was probably still doing from mine and ran away. I think he was probably much more satisfied with that surprise than he ever would have been from messing with my leg anyway. When Conway finally made his way to me a few minutes later, I noticed that he was as red as ever and when he stopped by me, he cussed a little, corrected his lips as usual, and then asked me if I wanted to take some crabs home to my family. Remember, I was a "come-here." I've had crab meat before; I've crabbed off of the pier before too, but that was for only one crab at a time.

I've even had those delicious crab sandwiches from the restaurant down the street, but never-ever have I gotten involved with a big bunch of the 'if-you-touch-me-I'll-pinch-you' kind of crabs. I wanted to act like a local, so I told Conway, "Sure, I'll take a crab." He then pulled a bushel basket of those things off the wagon he was pulling around and set them at my feet. I thanked him and he popped another top and went on his way. As I was looking at that bushel of crabs, I thought to myself, *I wanted a crab, not crabs*, and I definitely didn't want a whole bushel of those pinchy green bay critters. I didn't have a long walk to get home, but I didn't know how I was going to get there with all those killer crustaceans snapping at me all the way there either. I finally decided to be as brave as I could, and I picked up that basket of crabs to see how far I could get. I thought that was a good idea at the time but, like with most things, I was wrong once again.

I ended up spilling that bushel basket over almost immediately after I picked it up and all those crafty, little, green buggers went everywhere. They were scrambling all over the place and chasing me around backwards with their snappy pinchers stretched out in the air. Just like I was with Pogo, at this point, I just wanted to get away from those things, but they wouldn't let me. I felt like the pied piper of Crab Island, and I didn't even have to have a flute. That colony of crabs followed me about halfway home until, thank goodness, they decided to take a sharp left turn towards their first glimpse of the creek that led to the bay. I decided not to tell my grandparents that their brave grandson was bamboozled by a bunch of diabolically evil crabs but, once again, I realized that place didn't only have a bunch of colorful people, I guess it was proving itself to have some pretty colorful wildlife too. Ikey, the great and mighty lady's man, made it to our house soon after I did. This man was so happy, I guess from finding his own new best friend that he pulled out a harmonica, something else that no one knew he had or could even play, but, boy, could he play.

He sat on the front porch and blew on that little silver mouth harp so harmoniously loud that other campers started gathering around to see who it was that was blowing out those surprisingly pleasant sounds. If I had been smarter, I would have put a money bucket out, but I wasn't. At the time, a few people were checking in at the registration building across the dirt road. That building was only about twenty yards or so away and they obviously could hear the sweet music that old man was surprisingly permeating through the air. I guess their curiosity got the best of them too because they also came over to see who it was that was playing that tiny instrument so boldly. I bet they were surprised when they saw a tall, old, extremely tanned man, but it wasn't them who seemed to be the most surprised. Ikey and everyone else in the crowd almost froze when this one particular puffy-haired man came over.

This man's mere presence made Ikey stop playing altogether and the crowd itself tightened up around the man once he was in their presence. Ikey's once bronzed appearance turned to a more pale shade, almost like a normal person's. Then the man asked Ikey to play some more, so, more nervously than before, Ikey obliged and started playing again. It wasn't long before after he stated back that everyone noticed he was playing that thing even better than he did before. Little by little, Ikey not only got his groove back but, before long, someone went and got that mysterious, puffy-haired man a guitar and he started singing and playing along with Ikey. That man on the guitar could play, but his voice is what everyone was really in awe about. His beautiful voice sounded like velvet and no one wanted this newly-formed duo to stop anytime soon. Those men played and sang together for almost a solid hour.

They played long enough for almost everyone on the campground and the surrounding houses to gather around. This included my grandparents, Claire, and her parents too. When the men finally stopped, you would have thought they had just finished a concert at the Grand Ole' Opry with all the cheers and applause they drew. The puffy-haired man then told Ikey that he had to go but he greatly enjoyed their jam session. Now that Ikey gained most of his normal bronzeness back, in his eternal wisdom, he could only gather the words, "You too, man" as a response to that man's compliments.  That was twice that day, and probably in my life at that point, that I saw a man who was never short on words become almost speechless. His temporary lack of vocabulary was seemingly caused by two significant reasons. The first was, Miss Anna had also made her way to the crowd of onlookers and she saw our elderly celebrity in the making have his day in the sun. The second reason I learned after Ikey leaned down to ask me if I knew who that puffy-haired man was. I said, "No, but it's obvious he needed a haircut." Ikey laughed and said, "That's the king, man."

He told me that as excitedly as I'd ever heard him speak. *King? What king?* I sarcastically thought. King Richard, King Tutt, Burger King? "What king?" I asked. My grandfather and Ikey both always forgot how young I actually was. Ikey told me that the man who he just jammed out with was Elvis. I had no idea who Elvis was, but I did know he sure could sing and he also made Ikey very happy that day. *Between Miss Anna and Elvis, Ikey seemed to be having a well- deserved, pretty wonderful day,* I thought. Unfortunately for me, however, he spent the next hour telling me about why I should know who Elvis was. In reality, he was just proudly passing on a little more of his knowledge to one of his biggest fans once again. There was only one other time that a visitor to the campground made anyone as excited as Ikey was in playing his music with Elvis that day, and those people were Claire and I. We had been on the beach like we were on most days. We built sandcastles and played in the water as we usually did, but, as we finished on this one particular day, both of our mouths flung open as wide as they ever did from the astonishment at who we saw on our way home that day.

We ran over to this fat man who wasn't wearing any red, or even a shirt at all for that matter. He didn't have any reindeer with him, and he definitely wasn't at the North Pole because he was at our campground. After both of us started hugging him around his large, jiggly waist, we couldn't help but yell out, "Santa Claus, Santa Claus!" He was right there in front of us live and in color. *The Christmas season must have really worn him out that year because the North Pole had to be even farther away than Miss Anna's home country of Germany,* I thought. We'd seen large men there who looked like Santa before, heck, my grandfather wasn't too far off, but this was definitely the real Santa Claus and Claire and I both knew it. As we spoke to him, he was just as jolly and welcoming as we hoped he'd be. He confirmed that he was on vacation, sabbatical as he called it, and he loved Gwynn's Island and the campground just like we did.

I couldn't believe we were standing there talking to the real Santa Claus. We talked like we were all old friends, just jabbering about this and that. After both Claire and I got in a few years' worth of Christmas wishes, I guess his cookies must have been ready because Mrs. Claus called him in to eat. She didn't look anything like she did in the pictures though. She was a lot younger and she had blonde hair. I bet she could bake as well as Miss Anna because he didn't waste any time leaving when she called for him either. Before he left, however, he did give us both one last hug and told us to make sure we stayed off the naughty list. We promised and ran home to tell everyone who we saw that day. My grandmother listened attentively but my grandfather wanted to make sure the other big man didn't have any of his reindeer with him. I guess he was worried about having to pick up reindeer poop, but he didn't, so all was well. I still couldn't believe we saw the real Santa Claus and, even though it was July, I confidently asked my grandmother if we could put up our Christmas tree a little early out of respect.

I usually got my way with most things, but my grandmother couldn't quite see the sense in my request that time, Santa sighting or not. It didn't matter to me though. How many kids get to see the real Santa, or for that matter, have them stay at their grandparents' campground? That day was like when I rode on the bulldozer with my grandfather. My youthful chest was a little more pumped up. My grandmother interrupted what I had requested by saying she didn't want to hear anything about presents again for a while. She reminded us that Claire and I both just had our birthdays not that long ago and that was more than enough for a while. Ikey overheard my grandmother's conversation and blurted out, "Besides, mine is the next." I didn't think that when you got Ikey's age you wanted any more acknowledgments of another birthday but he evidentially did. My grandmother didn't say anything at the time, but she did have a plan about what Ikey had just revealed so loudly to everyone.

My grandmother was going to throw him a big birthday party on the day that he said his birthday was on. She went out and bought the pointy birthday hats and pink balloons. The balloons were my grandmother's attempt at a funny reminder about the pink culottes he had to wear after the "my-damn-tobacco" incident. To make sure he got the joke, she also bought him a toy dump truck and was planning to sit it straight up in the air on top of his birthday cake. She also baked his favorite cake, which as absolutely weird as it was, was fruit cake. I didn't think anyone's favorite cake was fruit cake but that crazy old man's was. When the day came, she invited all of his friends over to celebrate his special day. When his birthday came, she already knew how she was going to pull off the surprise. Ikey came over every Saturday afternoon to watch roller derby of all things. He said his television set couldn't tune into to that particular channel that roller derby came on. I think he really just wanted to be near us a little more, but no one minded anyway, so, after a while, it just became a habit.

Since she knew where he'd be, the date and time was set. As Ikey started to turn on the television that Saturday afternoon, everyone who was there jumped out and yelled surprise. He grinned from ear to ear in appreciation. His party made him almost as happy as he was when he played the harmonica with Elvis, but what helped substantiate his delight once again was Miss Anna was also in attendance. *Maybe this man really should be named Romeo P. Rolfe*, I thought. Miss Anna brought more of her Frisky Toodles, or whatever you call those delicious, sugary cinnamon biscuit treats with here too. Between the fruitcake and those cinnamon biscuit treats, Ikey was in a sugary heaven of sorts. I was surprised his face didn't turn as red as Conway's usually was, but it didn't. This was another truly amazing day for a truly amazing man. There was just one definite problem that would soon come to light.

When my grandmother asked Ikey how old he was, my ears perked up because I was expecting him to say something like a hundred forty-six or seven, but he didn't. Ikey just laughed as he wiped a few of the fruit cake crumbs from around the left corner of his mouth and the cinnamon and sugar off the right side. He then laughed and said, "I'll let you know when my birthday gets here." That man let everyone go through all that trouble without saying anything until it was all over. No one could be overly mad at Ikey, but my grandmother had to know why in the world he said it was his birthday when it wasn't. He laughed again a little harder and said, "I just wanted some fruit cake and more of those delicious sugary cinnamon treats." This was the most reasonable way for this sometimes-unreasonable man to get what he wanted. My grandmother laughed at his response and started cleaning up the party mess while shaking her head.

It took my grandfather a bit longer to catch on to what Ikey had just pulled off. When he did though, he laughed for about thirty minutes at Ikey's true reasoning for having a falsified birthday party. Birthday or not, it was a great party with some great people, and a few pretty wonderful treats just happened to be there too. I'm not saying that old tan man would lie to get something he wanted, but he did, and he did it more than once too. This time, that little white lie was for himself in a way but that really was a rarity, and it was also about cake and those sugary cinnamon biscuit treats, so it was kind of understandable to me. Most of the time, when Ikey stretched things out a bit, it usually ended up with someone else being in a much better position than they were before he so lovingly applied his own peculiar wisdom, or, sometimes, even fabrication to the matter.

# LEGENDS AND MYTHS

**A**s the weeks of the summer went by, our work and even playtime seemed to decrease because Claire and I always wanted more of Ikey's story time instead. We also definitely wanted the great adventures that so often came afterward. About a week after Ikey's not-birthday-party, his storytelling career really started to begin, and he got serious about it too. Ikey always talked about certain things that were so unbelievable that many of his stories were just fun to hear, but that was about it. Not this time though. This time, he was much more serious and way more believable too. One evening at about six o'clock in the evening, Ikey sat Claire and I down at our normal spot on the beach near the bay. He had a rare serious look on his face as he made it a point to ensure that we both paid full attention to everything he was about to tell us. As he proceeded, he told us that he wanted to tell us a secret, but it had to stay between just us and, if his secret ever got out, we'd scare away who the secret was about. Ikey made us both promise the most serious kind of promise of all—the pinky promise.

He made it clear that we'd have to swear that we'd never tell anyone, not even our friends or families before he'd begin. Claire and I looked at each other and then looked back at Ikey as to visually confirm his request, and then we finalized our agreement with a triple lock of our littlest fingers and a double nod from Claire and me. Ikey then started telling us the story of what he called, "Gwynn's Island's lady in the bay." Once he started, we couldn't get enough. Both Claire and I had seen the movie Pocahontas, we even studied her in school. We also vaguely remembered that she was the daughter of one of the most powerful Indian chiefs in history, Chief Powhatan. We both excitedly recalled that her tribe, the Powhatan Indians, inhabited all of the lands around Gwynn's Island long ago. With most of Ikey's other stories, he'd look in the air as if he was trying to find the words for the next thing he was going to make up, but not this time.

This time, he thoroughly knew every sentence that he was going to tell us as if it was genetically entrenched in his soul to do so. He told us it was his birthright not only to possess this story but also to pass it on to those who he felt were worthy enough and only to those he could trust the most. Claire and I were more than honored about being those people to our dear old friend. Ikey's deep blue eyes tensed up and even darkened a bit as he proudly reflected on what he felt he had to tell us. As he spoke, our grateful, young ears soaked up every single word that engaging old man was saying and now, acting out on the beach. He raised his hand and pointed to a buoy no more than a hundred yards out in the bay. He said, "That is where Pocahontas played in her long thatched canoe when she was a little girl. Right over there." She and some of the other young Indian children would often hunt for what they considered as treasures. He said, sometimes they would find shells, sand dollars, or even pearls.

On this one particular day, a terrible storm came up out of nowhere, as we all know happens in the bay area fairly often. This made the other Indian children head towards their homes like I'm sure they were supposed to, but not Pocahontas. Disney and all the history books had it right about her, she had a fiery spirit. She was very adventurous and being that way, she decided to play through the storm, even if it meant it had to be by herself. At the same time, a young military man named Colonel Hugh Gwynn was in the area fishing. Similar to Pocahontas, he also decided to wait the storm out in the bay. All of a sudden, and without warning, a tremendous bolt of lightning came crashing down and struck the tip of Pocahontas' canoe. It didn't take long for that little thatched vessel to become engulfed in flames, leaving Pocahontas with no other choice than to try to swim ashore. As hard as she tried, the storm was too fierce, the waves were too high and the undertow was too great. As the Indian child gasped her last breath of life, she gathered up enough strength to let out one final cry for help.

Colonel Gwynn heard the child's cries of distress and quickly made his way over to her. As he pulled the little girl in his boat, she was lifeless and limp. He feared he was too late, but Colonel Gwynn didn't give up. He shook her little shoulders and he pounded on her chest until, finally, she started spitting up what made her so lifeless in the first place. The trauma from the event left Pocahontas beyond exhausted, but she was alive. In those days, Colonial and Indian relations were questionable at best, but Colonel Gwynn did exactly what he would have wanted for his own daughter as he personally took the scared and tattered little girl to her father, the chief. Chief Powhatan was so relieved and thankful that his beloved daughter was safely back with him that he gave the Island near where all of this happened to the Colonel as a gift of gratitude for his honorable actions. Claire and I had a puzzled look on our face like we knew something that we didn't know before, but we just couldn't put our finger on exactly what that was.

Ikey, shook his head and muttered something about the youth of today and then said, "Think about it: Colonel Gwynn... Gwynn's Island." "Oh, now I get it!" I yelled out. Gwynn's Island was named after Colonel Hugh Gwynn and it was because he saved one of our country's most beloved and famous people from the past, Pocahontas. After our slow yet definite enlightenment set in, Ikey asked if we wanted to go get something to eat or take a break, but this story was just getting too good, so there was no way food—probably for the first time in my life—was going to get in the way. I don't think we would have left from hearing Ikey's story even if it were for more of Miss Anna's Frooble Doobles, or whatever you call those delicious, sugary cinnamon biscuit treats. After Ikey clearly heard that we didn't want to take a break, he told us about the many things that Pocahontas did during her lifetime. He spoke of the places she went, the people she met, and how much her life mattered to so many other people.

He also told us about her marriage to John Rolfe. Claire spoke up and said, "Hey, don't you mean, John--" but, before she could finish her sentence, Ikey quickly stopped her and said, "I said what I mean, and I mean John Rolfe." Ikey wasn't rude about it, he just seemed to know what he knew and wanted us to know it too. As Ikey's story went on, he gave credit to Colonel Gwynn and this beautiful Island for giving Pocahontas the chance to live the life that she was able to. His eyes saddened when he told us about how young she was when she died, but then brightened up again when he said, "Regardless of her age, she lived such a good life that she was able to pick where she went in the afterlife." To Pocahontas' tribe, the surrounding land and waters were their heavens, and this area was especially special to Pocahontas according to Ikey. Claire and I immediately started looking around. I figured, if we saw Elvis and Santa here, why not Pocahontas too?

Ikey knew what we were doing and let us childishly glance around for a while, then laughed at us as he often did. After that revelation he asked us to follow him to the edge of that beautiful Chesapeake Bay. He, once again, pointed out to the bay, but this time, the aim of where he was directing us to look was even more pronounced than when my grandmother wanted me to look at that stupid skate that stuck its tongue out at me. Ikey repeated himself and said again, and more clearly this time, "She's out there. Our own lady in the bay is out there, in the water." This was one of those times where, at least at first, I thought maybe he was going back to some of his old made-up ways, but this time was different, it really was. Ikey told this story much differently than he did any other. Besides, before I had a chance to doubt him anymore, I saw a ripple in the water near where he was pointing, and Claire said she she saw it too. That swirl that seemed to be made on cue caused me to totally forget about questioning the validity of his story in any way. I'm not saying that it was the lady in the bay, but I'm not saying it wasn't either, but I definitely thought it kind of looked like it could have been.

As we sat back down on the beach, Ikey said he wanted to explain just a bit more before we really had to go this time. Before we knew it, it was almost dinner time and time to take another whack at that giant skate with my grandmother. Before we had to leave, in Ikey's closing remarks, he explained that Pocahontas chose the waters near Gwynn's Island as her final resting place so she could help the people of the area the same way that she was helped so many years ago. Ikey said, if we ever needed her, all we had to do was believe that she exists, keep his secret, and to wholeheartedly seek her out. He then reminded us again that this secret was just for us, the only people he thought were worthy enough, as he put it, for him to tell his birthright to. I think both Claire and I were thinking about all the times that we thought we saw or heard something in the water. I know I was. Could this story really be true? Is Pocahontas out there, and is she really our own lady in the bay? A million questions rambled through my mind after hearing the best story I had ever heard in my life.

For a second, I thought about asking if that Pocahontas protectionary plan applies to the come-here's too. Before I did though, I figured for myself that, if I was worthy enough to hear Ikey's story, then I must also be included in that potential gift. Ikey more or less dismissed us after that. We hugged and thanked him for entrusting us with his secret story and started on our way home. As Claire and I were walking towards my house, she looked over at me and, out of the blue, asked me what Ikey's last name was. I had to reach back in my small memory bank, but when the answer finally came to me, my jaw slung open even wider than it did before. After I told her that Ikey's last name was Rolfe, I think Claire's jaw surpassed mine. We both knew we had another confirmation about the actual truthfulness of Ikey's wonderful secret story and we were so excited about where we both knew it was going to take us.

Claire went home to eat with her parents after our evening on the beach with Ikey and I did the same with my grandparents. As I was sitting at the dinner table, I wanted to talk about what Ikey told us earlier that day so badly, but I didn't. I promised to keep his secret and, by then, I was also pretty hungry, so food took a pretty good chunk of my thinking space away. That night, when my grandmother and I went fishing, we didn't get a bite or even see anything close to a skate, but it was the first time I ever kept anything from her, and, to be perfectly honest, I felt kind of guilty. I didn't tell her about Ikey's secret, but I definitely wanted to. Even more than that though, I wanted the people that I loved so much to be as protected by the lady in the bay as Ikey said Claire and I were if we found her. The next morning, when I met Claire, I told her about what I was thinking, and she not only agreed with me but said she was feeling the same way about her parents, and was somewhat bothered by those feelings as well. We both wanted that same protection for our families. The question we had for ourselves was, how could we help both of our families know about the lady in the bay without directly telling them about her?

Youth really is a magical time. As adults, life and all of the obligations and responsibilities often cloud your imagination, but not when you're young. I think it was Albert Einstein who said, "Imagination is more important than knowledge because knowledge is limited, but you're the only one who can limit your imagination." It was obvious that Claire and I were taking Mr. Einstein's views about imagination to heart because we took Ikey's story and embellished it ourselves with our own imaginations. We even made something out of it that Ikey may have never guessed we would, or would he? We knew we had to keep Ikey's secret, but Claire and I were both feeling that we had to include the ones we loved the most as much as we wanted to find her for ourselves. These thoughts were tricky because we knew we had to figure out a way under the very special pinky promised circumstances too.

Claire and I never questioned that there was only one place we could do that much thinking, and that place was what we not-so-creatively named Fort Fishing Shack. That little shack was probably as old as Ikey was, but my grandfather still put a new blue metal roof on it for some reason. When he started working, he never knew when to stop, so, often times, he'd do what my grandmother comically called, "putting lipstick on a pig." In other words, he'd pretty up something that couldn't ever be but so pretty again. That tiny shack had a hole in the floor that could be used to drop a line through if we wanted to fish when it was cold outside. It also had these long shelves mounted on each wall with a sink in the middle of the shelf that was the farthest away from the door. It was the side most commonly used for cleaning fish and the side that, understandably, stunk the most too. Regardless of the horrid smell, it was one of the few places that hardly anyone else ever went to.

That exclusivity made it a popular spot for Claire and me, especially when we had some things to figure out. Some of our best ideas throughout the years originated in that smelly, little shack and we felt we needed to use it this time as much as ever, if not more. Claire had a different way of figuring things out than I did though. She'd write all of her ideas down on paper and scratch through the ones that we voted out. If she, or, in some cases, we liked the plan, she'd put a check mark beside it. When she thought the plan was a really good one, she'd then draw a heart around it too. It wasn't a very complicated system, but I have to admit, it seemed to work for us as well as anything did throughout our youth. Claire's planning always seemed to work better than my method anyhow. What I'd usually do would be to just blurt out whatever I was thinking while she, more times than not, stood there shaking her head at me in disapproval about most of my solo ideas. As she began to write our ideas down, this time in our adolescent way of thinking, I guess we compared finding Pocahontas to fishing.

Maybe it was something that we thought we already understood pretty well, so, similarly, we thought if we offered Pocahontas some food, then maybe she'd take the bait. To confirm this possibility, Claire checked off our newly conspired plan and drew a bright-red heart around it for the absolute confirmation of it being the best possible direction for us to proceed. She added to our plan that she'd always have a camera with her just in case. She also checked and hearted that supplemental idea too. We just knew, if everything worked out the way we thought it would, we could keep our promises to Ikey and, even better than that, if we got a picture of the lady in the bay to boot while, more or less, fishing for her, our families would have to believe that she was real too. She could always be there for them if they ever needed her as well. We just knew our plan would work because Ikey said all we needed to do was believe she exists, keep his secret, and to wholeheartedly seek her out.

To Claire and I, we were already at that point, so we became almost giddy at what we just knew we were getting ready to accomplish together for the well-being of both of our families. Claire walked out of the shack first but, before I shut the door behind us, I looked up at what I knew about God at the time and thanked him. I've done that since that day, but that was the first time I can remember doing it when I was younger. Meeting that little blonde girl changed my life, and I was beginning to realize that there are some people who come into your life who just seem to fit, no matter what age you are, or what you've ever been through; you just know, as unexplainable as it may be, they are a predestined gift from above. Claire was that for me and I always knew I was that for her too. My heart smiled as I closed the door to our little Fort Fishing Shack and we both headed out towards our new, confidently-hearted mission. There were only a few things that we really weren't allowed to do back then, being that we were so young, one of those limitations was going out in a boat by ourselves.

We had to be with an adult or stay on dry land. That rule was written in stone and one that we both knew we better never break. The thing is, no one ever said we couldn't go out with Conway the Crab Man, who just happened to go out in that beautiful bay every single day. We figured there was no way that Conway could refuse a request from two cute little kids. As long as he didn't have a problem with taking us with him, we felt that we had just about every part of our plan set to perfection. We did, however, have two little issues and one very big, grey, three-legged problem. The first was, neither Claire nor I had a clue about what Pocahontas liked to eat. The second issue was that we knew Conway usually left long before we ever woke up. The third, much bigger, potentially much worse issue was that doggone dog, Pogo. He was always with Conway and we knew he'd be there on the day we wanted to go too.

These little issues required just a little more thinking but, before long, we had what we thought were the final answers and, once again, to prove its brilliance, Claire had it all checked and hearted to perfection. This time, Claire and I felt we definitely came up with the most perfectly complete solution to all of our problems. The first heart was somewhat easy. We knew that Conway left long before we'd usually wake up, so, in order to catch him before he left, we'd have to get up that early too. The second and third hearts I was especially proud of because I came up with them myself and they both involved the same solution. My solution meant we'd be visiting Miss Anna once again in hopes of getting some more of those Fligglesnozzles, or whatever you call those delicious, sugary cinnamon biscuit treats that she loves to make so much and the one's we, and hopefully Pocahontas love to eat. Miss Anna was more than happy to bake some more of those delicious biscuit things for us, and she even said she'd make a little extra so we could take a few plates back to our families. This offering of excess played perfectly into all that we were planning without us even trying very hard.

We knew our families would miss out on those delicious snacks but Pogo and Pocahontas surely wouldn't. As we waited for our bait to finish baking, she told us that she had a nephew who would be coming to visit her in a few weeks. He was a little boy named Jonas. She said Jonas was around our age and she asked if we would show him around the campground while he was there. Claire and I always welcomed any company, and if he was as nice as Miss Anna, then we could hardly wait until he got there. After hearing the news of possibly having another running mate, I started thinking about Germany. All I really knew about the place was they have some pretty terrific desserts and, from what I've seen in pictures, they make their children wear some kind of ridiculous-looking bib overall short pants. I think they're called lederhosen or something like that but, for some reason, they always seem to be brown or greenish in color. Those overalls look to be even shorter than my grandmother's pink pants were on Ikey's lanky, old brown body that time. I started giggling to myself thinking about that day.

That's one of the many memories of that old man that will forever be lovingly and comically stamped in my mind. How many people have a story about two old men trying to launch a dump truck in the air any way, I thought? After our bait was kept in a safe place overnight, Claire and I woke up really-really early in the morning. We knew we had to intercept The Crab Man on his way out. We felt, without question, that we had come up with the perfect bait to keep Pogo off of our legs and hopefully lure Pocahontas, AKA, The Lady in the Bay in the boat with us. As Conway was walking towards the pier, we ran over and joined him. Claire snuck over to his left side and I went to the right. We both looked up at him with our best version of pouty puppy dog eyes. Claire's were much more convincing than mine were, I'm sure, but I was trying too. After that the Crab Man didn't mind taking us with him at all.

He even made sure he didn't drink as much as he usually did. To prove that fact, I think he only had about two or three of those Coors Lights for breakfast, and not many more than that for lunch. As we bounced through the waves, Claire was originally on Pocahontas duty by herself while my responsibility was to handle Pogo the pumper. Claire wrapped a string around a biscuit just like we'd do with a chicken neck or fish head when we crabbed off of the pier. In truth, at that time, we weren't fully convinced that our bait was going to work on the Lady in the Bay or not, but they sure did do the trick on Pogo. That dog ate so many of those sugary cinnamon biscuit treats that he, thankfully, slept for the whole trip after he finished gobbling up a half dozen or so. His stomach was evidently so full that all we heard out of him after his feast was just a little whimper every now and then. I'm guessing he was either dreaming about more of those biscuit treats or he may have even had a bellyache from eating too many of them as fast as he did.

Either way, that part of the plan was working without a hitch. Once Conway stopped the boat, he began to pull in his crab pots from the port side, and Claire and I began our secret mission on the starboard side of the boat. As we lowered our weighted biscuit-laden lines down into the water, nothing happened at first. We understood the wait because we often had to wait quite a while for our first bite during many of the times we went fishing or crabbing with my grandmother too. Knowing there is often a slow start to such an endeavor, I told Claire that we just needed to stay positive, be patient and keep to our task. *I was sounding more and more like my grandfather,* I thought to myself as I shook my head at my own self that time. Then, a thought came over me. When my grandmother noticed that I was getting a little antsy from not catching fish as fast as I thought I should be, she'd often start singing in hopes of stirring up their interest in whatever it was we had to offer. She'd always lead the way and then invite me to join in as she'd sing, "Fishy, fishy in the bay, please, please jump on my hook today."

There were many times I thought maybe she had gotten into some of Conway's libations herself but, believe it or not, her songs worked more often than not. It was so much fun watching her sing to the fish that it didn't matter to me how silly I may have looked. I always ended up joining in with my grandmother on a few verses of my own. I think Claire wanted to check my blood alcohol level to see if I tested out what was inside of Conway's silver cans after I told her about what worked for me and my grandmother, especially after I led the way with the first verse. At first, she just laughed at me, but she ended up having so much fun watching and listening to me sing to the Lady in the Bay that she didn't bother giving my sobriety another thought and joined in herself. Instead of starting out with "Fishy, fishy in the bay," I did what my grandfather taught me, and I improvised. I started our little song by belting out "Lady, lady in the bay, won't you please, please take our sugary cinnamon biscuit treats today." We laughed and laughed as we sang our ridiculous version of my grandmother's song. Even though he didn't have a clue what we were singing about, Conway comically joined in with us. Once again, my grandmother's advice, even if it was slightly altered, began to work that time too.

Similarly to how that giant skate took my bait, I felt a big tug on my string and Claire said she felt a good size bite on hers too. We both started slowly pulling in our homemade rigs in hopes of not spooking away whatever it was that was tugging on it from below. Water seems to make everything feel lighter, so we couldn't tell if what was down there was big enough to be our promised protector or not but there was definitely something on both of our lines. Once we gingerly redirected the way our lines were coming in, we both felt something, or, hopefully, someone definitely getting ready to surface. We were ready too. Claire had her camera in one hand and her fishing rig in the other while I reached for some more of those sugary cinnamon biscuit treats, just in case the Lady in the Bay needed a little more incentive to join us.

As we brought our lines up, Conway's eyes brightened, much more than usual, as he yelled out, "Thanks!" to both Claire and I. His appreciation came from seeing that our lines, which were completely tangled up by then, had more crabs nibbling on our combined pile of soggy biscuits than any of his professionally made crab pots had in them. I guess crabs like those German treats as much we did because, there I was, once again, with those green pinchy things snapping up at me. We stayed out for quite a while that day but, instead of ever pulling in the Lady in the Bay, each time we lowered our biscuit bait into the water, we'd end up with more and more of those crabs on the other end. It seemed that Conway was the only one who had a successful day in terms of catching what he set out for. After seeing what he thought was our success, he had to know where we got our doughy dessert bait from. I guess Miss Anna has another fan of those tasty Frankenfurter dessert things, or whatever you call those crab-catching, dog-napping, wonderful German biscuit treats. Other than the increased haul, Conway seemed to truly appreciate our company as well. With Pogo still dead asleep, he drove us around the Island to show us a side of that beautiful place that we rarely got to see.

He was so appreciative of our day's catch that, from what I can remember, he only cussed once during the whole day. He did that time, on accident—according to him and his lips. On that occasion he called some man who had his boat anchored too close to one of his crab pots an ass cracker. I didn't know exactly what an ass cracker was, but I'm pretty sure I didn't want any of them, nor would I like to be one either. After the cracker explicative, Conway showed us a fishing spot that he called "Wolf Trap," and then another that he said was named, "The Hole in the Wall." That was where the rivers and creeks actually poured into that glorious Chesapeake Bay and also where the water became quite a bit deeper in most spots. As we went around the campground, we saw the beach that Claire and I spent so much time on from the waterside.

We also got to see many of the other places from a completely different view. It was even more beautiful than it was from the land, and, after a short boat ride, we passed the Marina with all these huge yachts and sailboats. All of a sudden and without warning, we came to a complete stop in the water. It shook Conway's little boat and us inside of it quite a bit but, thankfully, not enough to wake up that dumb dog. We stopped right before we went underneath the swing bridge that we usually drove over when arriving to the Island. Even if I was asleep on the ride down, the roar of the grids coming across that big metal bridge always served as a gentle alarm clock telling me it was almost time—we were almost at Camper's Haven. A haven is defined as a place of safety and refuge. One thing was for sure, when I arrived, I didn't always feel safe because of my grandfather's little projects but I sure did feel like that haven or refuge was as close to heaven as I ever knew heaven to be. Even though Conway had a fairly small fishing boat, the man on the top of the bridge opened that giant structure as if we were passing through on the largest and most prestigious ship to ever sail the bay. The man from above smiled, blew this loud horn and waved at us as the bridge slowly swung open.

We felt like admirals of the sea as we went under where the bridge once was. Conway smiled too as to say, "Kids, this one's for you." Anyone who has experienced the roar of that bridge when crossing can see why Gwynn's Island is such a special place. It's almost like going back to a different era, to a more peaceful and relaxing time when people didn't mind doing that little extra for another. As soon as we cleared the bridge, there was a small restaurant on the left-hand side; Conway told us that it was also named, "The Hole in the Wall." I'm pretty sure it was named that because you could see the Hole in the Wall fishing spot from there but, either way, that's where we were headed. I actually had eaten there a few times with my family, and I knew they had the best crab cake sandwiches in the area—probably even the best in the country.

It was my favorite kind of crab too. The kind that couldn't pinch you or chase you around anymore because, they were in a sandwich now. As Conway made a pit stop at that little place, a nice lady came out to meet us at their pier. Conway then unloaded several bushels of crabs that were probably caught with our German biscuit bait on the pier. After he did, the lady called a younger guy over to take the crabs inside the restaurant. As she was leaving to go back inside, I guess to begin preparing them for the dinner crowd, she then turned to us and said the strangest thing as we were leaving. She thanked us for the crabs but then she ended our delivery by saying, "May the Lady in the Bay always bless you on your way," then she walked up the restaurant's wooden stairs and out of sight. *What a minute*, I thought, *did Ikey also tell her about our secret story too? What's going on here?* I looked at Claire to make sure she heard the same thing I did and, once she confirmed that she did, we both felt like we had another absolute confirmation about the truth of Ikey's story, even if we didn't catch her that day. Claire and I began to whisper to each other trying to figure out how the lady at the restaurant could have possibly known about the Lady in the Bay too.

Conway was still limiting his thirst, but he did have another beer in his hand at that point, so he wasn't really paying any attention to what we were doing or saying anyway. We may not have seen Pocahontas that day, but we were definitely getting closer to discovering more clues about her at a minimum. After talking about it quite a bit, we concluded that, since the lady at the restaurant was most likely a local herself, maybe she already knew the story as well. I didn't think that even Ikey could make up something that other people openly knew and even spoke about. So, even though Claire and I didn't see Pocahontas we were more hooked on the possibilities of Ikey's story than ever. From there, we made a few more stops on the way home.

# NIPPLE TOOTH

**A**lmost every time we pulled out of somewhere else, there was someone there wishing us that same farewell? One by one, everyone we made a delivery to wished us off by saying, "May the Lady in the Bay always bless you on your way." This was just too much of a coincidence not to be true. To top the day off in assuredness, as we pulled into the pier at the campground, we found a final piece of evidence that made the Lady in the Bay as real as anything that our young minds had ever known. As Claire and I stepped off the pier and reached the sand, there it was, the conclusive evidence about who we were looking for. Claire reached down and picked up an old necklace that definitely wasn't there when we left. It was so beautiful and, like our old, tan friend, extremely unique too. It was made out of these sparkling seashells, brilliant white sand dollars, and it had several stone-colored arrowheads attached to it in various places. All of the precious parts were tied together by an aged leather band, which, if it could talk, had to have more stories than even Ikey did, I thought.

Our newest discovery looked as if it just recently washed ashore but neither Claire nor I had any idea how it made it all the way up to the beginning of the pier and not somewhere closer to the water line on the beach. That beautiful necklace was the final clue that we needed about the realness of the Lady in the Bay and all that Ikey had so graciously entrusted us with. Claire and I just knew it had to be Pocahontas' because you just don't find something like that every day, or really any day for that matter, especially after going out all day looking for her as we had. We thought maybe she was leaving us a signal or some kind of a gesture for us to keep seeking her out, as if we weren't planning to do just that. As Claire put what we both knew was Pocahontas' necklace in the bag, the same bag that once contained our overly-successful, doughy crab bait, we both knew all of these signs and signals were just too perfect to be any kind of coincidence or just another loving fabrication from Ikey.

After we thanked Conway for taking us out with him, and for Pogo staying asleep during the trip, Ikey was the first one to meet us on our way home. He was always out and about anyway, so that made sense; besides, he told us that my grandfather was headed to the landfill in the dump truck so we understood why he'd be as far in the opposite direction as he could be for a while. As we were walking, we didn't think it was time to fully divulge the happenings of our day to Ikey. We didn't think we should tell him anything yet because, in our somewhat simple way of thinking, we didn't want to take a chance on him taking back his protectionary promise from the Lady in the Bay. We could still tell, however, that he was fishing for something himself. He asked about our trip and the rigs that we had thrown over our shoulders, the same ones that we actually used quite a bit that day in our attempts at catching something other than crabs for Conway. Regardless of his questioning, Claire and I admitted to going crabbing with Conway, and that was it. Technically, that's all we did anyway, and then I tried to change the subject, as kids our age often do.

No matter what my efforts were in avoiding Ikey's questions, he kept them coming in at us. He then directly asked us if we'd seen the Lady in the Bay while we were out with Conway. Neither Claire nor I admitted to anything. The main reason was, we simply didn't know exactly how close we ever really were to her. Again, in my attempt to talk about something else, I decided to ask a few questions of my own and, in doing so, try to take some of the prying pressure off of us. I knew there was supposed to be a new museum opening up on the Island soon, so I asked Ikey if he minded taking us to the grand opening, which I knew was just a day or two away. Ikey quickly forgot what he was originally asking us about and seemed more excited about going to the new museum than we were pretending to be. So, that was a definite and easy yes from him and a good way to change the subject away from his gentle interrogation.

Once we found out that the new museum would be opening for the first time the very next day, we made our plans to go. Claire and I went to our respective houses but Ikey still stayed as far away from where he thought my grandfather and his dump truck might be for the rest of the day. His avoidance didn't last that long though because, the next day, Ikey arrived back at our house almost as early as Claire and I left for our Pocahontas fishing trip the day before. We had to wait quite a while for Claire to get there but, once she did, Ikey and I both noticed she was all primped up in her church clothes as if she was knew something very special was going to happen that day. Once again, I dressed appropriately; I wore shorts, a t-shirt and tennis shoes. When we pulled up to the museum, I noticed that the exterior of the building looked pretty much like a regular house would in the area. It was a tall, white, two-story building with just a few steps underneath a blue overhang at the entrance. Regardless of its unimposing features from the outside, once we got inside, it was as intriguing as so many other sights are on that magnificent island.

As the three of us looked around, we saw so many historical collections from the past. That museum's collection even included a very unexpected Mastodon tusk for some reason. At first, I thought the word Mastodon was just a fancy way of saying Wooley Mammoth but the director of the museum quickly corrected my assumption. She then began telling me and the rest of my party about the many differences. She told us that the word Mastodon literally translated into the words, "Nipple Tooth." I looked at Ikey and shook my head as he smiled back at me. I tried to prepare Claire for what I knew was going to happen next. From knowing Ikey so well, I knew, without a doubt, that after hearing those two funny words together, he just couldn't and wouldn't resist. Our elderly wannabe comedian lived up to my expectations too, and for the rest of the visit, he acted like he was live at The Apollo.

Claire got a little embarrassed, but I knew what was getting ready to come from our much older, sometimes more immature, tanned chaperone, so I did the best I could to ignore him. Besides, we were supposed to be looking for clues. Ikey laughed and repeated the lady's words over and over again throughout the day, just like I knew he'd do. "Nipple tooth, Nipple tooth," he said over and over again. Then, he childishly asked, "Why in the world would anything that was related to a Wooley Mammoth be called a Nipple Tooth anyway?" He said, "Something so silly-sounding deserves to be made fun of," as he kept doing exactly that. We could tell the lady at the museum was getting a little frustrated with him. I'm sure she had never met anyone quite like Ikey before, but I knew not many people have. Regardless of Ikey's attempts to shake her, she just kept calmly explaining all the differences between the two pre-historic mammals. Come to find out, even Thomas Jefferson collected Mastodon bones, and, supposedly, those massive animals inhabited our little island at one time in history. I wanted to ask Ikey if he ever had a pet Mastodon, and I should have, but I didn't. The most interesting part of the visit for us, considering our current quest, was all the Native American items that were so well protected underneath the museum's many glass cases.

There were plenty of arrowheads and ancient sand dollars like the ones on the necklace we had just found the day before. Claire shook my shoulder to get my attention when no one was looking and when Ikey had the lady from the museum more than a little pre-occupied. She pointed out that there was a portion of a small thatched canoe in the corner. When we went over to inspect it closer, we felt that we found another definite clue. It looked as if the other parts of that historical homemade boat, the parts that weren't there, were burnt off in some way. We must have spent half of a day looking around in wonderment but also secretly searching for additional clues that would help us on our own search for someone historical.

Before we left, the nice lady who put up with Ikey saying "Nipple Tooth, Nipple Tooth" all day told us there were a few more exhibits upstairs, but they weren't quite ready for the general public to see. I think what she was really saying was she was ready for Ikey to leave, but, if we hurried, Claire and I could go up and take a quick look around. I don't know if the lady didn't want to correct Ikey in front of us, or why she pulled him aside to talk after we started upstairs, but that's what happened. As we left him to fend for himself, we began to notice the upstairs of that place was just as magnificent as the first floor. Since I felt Ikey was getting what he deserved, Claire and I took a little more time upstairs than we probably should have. Once we were up there, though, there was no question that we were seeing both Pocahontas and Colonel Gwynn right there, face-to-face with us.

Surprisingly enough, there was a statue of each standing together in one of the rooms on the second floor. It was almost as if they were waiting for us to meet them there. They were what I'd describe as exact replicas of everything that we knew about them. Claire and I just knew that the statues were another definite confirmation that we seemed to be mysteriously receiving from everywhere in the universe. It all kept adding up to make us completely feel like it was a mission that both of us were meant to be on. Ikey's story, his last name, the farewells from the locals, the necklace that Claire found, the half of a canoe, and now the other Native American artifacts and statues from the new museum. It was definitely clearer than ever that it was our duty to find Pocahontas and, in doing so, the Lady in the Bay with her. As we left, Ikey, just like he was doing all day said, "Nipple Tooth, Nipple Tooth" one more time, and the nice, extremely patient lady from the museum ended our visit by letting out that now-familiar final farewell: "May The Lady in the Bay always bless you on your way."

We may not have ever had what any sane person would call a "normal" day back then but I can't remember a day that wasn't fun, and almost every day had so many unexpected happenings no matter what we were doing or where we went. There's more than just an innocence when you look at life through the eyes of a child. I believe there's more clarity of how life was meant to be lived. In being childlike, regardless of what age you actually are there doesn't seem to be the stress or self-imposed struggle that so many seem to create in their own lives. There's only room for imagination, wonderment and visions of life's great possibilities. Those possibilities are what our Mr. Nipple Tooth obviously always saw in everything. I'm sure glad he was such a big part of my life, even if he was quite embarrassing at times. Before we made it all the way home, Ikey asked us if we had ever heard the story of the sand dollar. I guess seeing so many sand dollars at the museum that day sparked something in him that he felt he needed to get out to his young fan club.

Not only did we just see quite a few sand dollars, we just found a necklace full of them, which we were still trying to hide from him and everyone else for the time being. Claire shook her head almost immediately as to signal to Ikey that she'd never heard that particular story before. For me, to be completely honest, I had heard a story about a sand dollar at church a few months back but, no matter what I may have heard in the past, I had no idea what Ikey's version of the story would be, so I joined in with Claire and shook my head no as well. With what I heard from the preacher, the five slashes on a sand dollar represent the wounds that Christ suffered on the cross at Calvary. Four slashes came from the stakes that were driven through Jesus' wrists and the tops of his feet, nearer to his ankles. The fifth was the wound that a Roman soldier put in the side of his chest with a spear. That last stab was to ensure that he was actually dead after the crucifixion. I also learned that there was somehow a star stamped on the top of each sand dollar.

That star was described that Sunday at church as the most perfectly symmetrical shape that ever existed. It was also described as a symbol of the star of Bethlehem, which was what the wise men followed to find the newborn baby Jesus. As the preacher spoke, he told the congregation that if you break a sand dollar open, inside, you'll find what strongly resembles five white doves. According to him, the doves were all symbols of the love that was left behind ever since that holy arrival. I can remember really paying attention in church that day because, similar to when Ikey told us about the Lady in the Bay, it was all just so relatable, almost as if I could see it myself. I have to admit, Ikey began his new story in somewhat of a similar fashion but, like with most things, he started from the inside out. Ikey, did say there were five doves inside each and every sand dollar like the preacher did, but in Ikey's version, only one of the doves, the largest one, represented love. The other four stood for what he called "the key virtues to live by" according to his ancestors.

The four other doves, or virtues, according to his ancestors, stood for forgiveness, courage, empathy and grace and the star, had a completely different meaning in Ikey's rendition. It represented home according to Ikey, which was kind of confusing to me. As he spoke, he gave an example of each of the virtues, starting with the two that Claire and I already kind of knew about—forgiveness and courage. We definitely needed a little more clarity on the other two doves and the star though. Ikey explained empathy by telling us it meant having the ability to be able to relate to someone else's feelings, even if you don't completely agree with them. It's like putting yourself in someone else's shoes or understanding what it's like to walk their life's path as he said. That seemed simple enough, but his definition of grace sounded even better to me. Ikey told us that grace was like being able to eat your dessert without having to finish your vegetables first.

It was learning how to accept gifts that you didn't earn or even deserve in some cases but having the ability to realize those gifts or blessings didn't necessarily have anything to do with our own efforts. I wasn't completely sure at that time what he was talking about, but grace sure sounded good to me; I like dessert first. Then he told us that the biggest of the doves, the dove of love, always led the other virtues and that we'd all have times in life where the biggest dove may seem to be hiding, but, even if we couldn't see it or feel it, it would always be there. This was a lot for a couple of kids to take in all at once so we didn't push him any further in explaining what the star of home meant so once again, I tried to change the subject. Ikey must have felt we had had enough for the day because then he said, "There you have it. There are the twelve reminders from a sand dollar." I was mentally saturated at this point but, once again, thinking I knew something that I didn't before and not being completely sure what that was, I started counting on my fingers to try and figure out exactly what that was.

I thought to myself, *five doves and a star make six, and then there are five slots on the front of a sand dollar, which, if I added them all together, only made eleven.* I thought to myself, *Ikey just said there were twelve reminders in a sand dollar, and I counted out only eleven.* So, in absolute confidence, and probably trying to show off a little in front if Claire, I blurted out, "Where's the twelfth?" Ikey laughed at my rare perception of things and said, "On the front side of every sand dollar you'll also see an imprint of a flower." He started laughing even harder as he said, "And that's the great reminder to never forget to bring your sweetheart flowers." I think he had me up until the 'bring your sweetheart flowers' part. The imprint on the front of a sand dollar really does look like a flower but *come on, man,* I thought. I guess his story had reminded him that he needed to bring Miss Anna some flowers and he conveniently added it to his version of the sand dollar story to solidify that remembrance.

On the way home, we stopped by that little country store again. That was the same store where I first met our friendly storyteller, and now that his story reminded him that he needed to get some flowers for Miss Anna, I guess that's where we had to go again. As he got out of the truck, Claire and I were going to wait for him until he got back but he had plans of his own for me. Instead of letting me wait with Claire, he waved me inside with him. Once I reached where he was, he didn't waste any time with his selection. He had what he needed and what he thought I needed too. After he paid the lady at the register, that strange old man kept one bunch of the lilies in his left hand and handed me the other bunch with his right hand. He winked at me while he did it too. He'd always wink at me whenever he was trying to punctuate whatever point he was trying to make, and this time he did it again. I didn't wink back though, I squinted back at him and turned my head to the side a bit as if to ask, why in the world are you giving me these flowers? I can remember thinking, *I'm not your sweetheart, you crazy old man.*

To me, those flowers were extremely similar to that jet-black bug killer and I didn't want any part of either one of them. Ikey's eyes gave me another non-verbal signal back and forth towards Claire who was still patiently waiting for us in the truck. He probably did that a half dozen times or more before I finally picked up on the message he was trying to send out about what he thought I should do. I wasn't shy anymore around Claire at all. I even sang to the Lady in the Bay, or crabs, in our case, in front of her but I never thought about giving her any kind of a representation of our closeness before. As I opened the truck door and handed the second bunch of lilies to Claire, she blushed and I, unexpectedly and embarrassingly, started flubbering my words all around again like I did the first I time I heard her beautiful, little, soul-soothing voice. I was even stuttering the words that I was thinking to myself in my own mind.

I'd never given flowers to a girl before and I really didn't know why I was doing it then, even if they were for who I thought was the best girl in the world. In our youthful relationship, we each knew how we felt about one another but we never talked about it, and we absolutely never traded any kind of gift to show our sprouting connectedness before. Ikey, for the third time in his life, was speechless. The first time was when he met Miss Anna, the second was when he played his harmonica with Elvis, and now this time on the way home from Scrooch's country store. I think this time he was as quiet as he was just to see what he could hear out of us, but he didn't hear much. Neither Claire nor I said another word all the way home. She just smiled and I sat there as discombobulated as I've ever been. I really was secretly glad Ikey pushed me into giving Claire a present but it made me realize even more than ever that I always hoped she'd be in my life, and to my adolescent self, I truly meant forever.

After we got home, Claire smiled at both of us and hugged us both around the neck one by one, hugging me first. She then did something I'd never seen her do before: she skipped all the way home. The romance master, Romeo P. Rolfe, took his half of the flowers and headed to Miss Anna's as fast as he could. I could swear that crazy old man was skipping on his way to her house as well. I, however, did something completely different. I went home and locked myself in my room. I didn't hide in my room because there was anything wrong; it was quite the opposite. I just didn't know how to handle my ever-growing youthful emotions. I think I went to my room in such a way because I was as happy as I'd ever been and just as much as the other two outwardly appeared to be, but I didn't want anyone to see me dancing around pretending like I was much braver than I actually was. Locked in my room, I relived the moment where I gave Claire the lilies a hundred times or more to myself. Each time I did it, I did it as if she was right there with me, even though it was only in my mind.

I made sure that during each one of those dramatizations, I was much smoother and a lot more confident than I was anywhere close to being when I should have been. I got to the point where I fictitiously made up how I handled the situation so much that I actually started believing that what I was pretending was actually the way it really happened. Maybe that's where the phrase "fake it until you make it" comes from because I was surely faking it by myself in my locked room. It's funny and weird at the same time that I wouldn't let my true joy out until the person I was most joyous about was at safe distance away from me and I was all alone. This young love stuff is so confusing. A week or so went by after our visit to the museum and then to Scrooch's little country store.

Claire and I searched for The Lady in the Bay quite a bit after that day, but it didn't seem to be as big of a priority as it was before the lilies. Even with all of the newly-found clues that were still coming in from everywhere, we had growing up consume our minds quite a bit more than before. Even though I didn't completely understand what was going on, I did know as much as ever that there are some people who come into your life that just seem to fit, no matter what age you are, or what you've ever been through. You just know they are, as unexplainable as it may be, a predestined gift from above. Claire was that for me and I always knew I was that for her too.

# CASTAWAYS

**B**ack then, if Claire was with us on our fishing evenings, my grandmother would sometimes leave us on the pier for a little longer by ourselves after she went inside. During most of that time, we'd lie on our backs and look up at what seemed like millions of stars shining down over us. Our stargazing always seemed to end up with us taking turns wishing on the brightest star we could find. Up until this point, the majority of our wishes had something to do with finding the Lady in the Bay but, after the lilies, Claire's wishes seemed to change, and, if I was honest with myself, mine did too. Again, this was innocent, but it was still a very special youthful love that we were sharing. This was as real of a love to us as we knew love to be, especially after I heard Claire wish that we'd always remember what we meant to each other so many times while lying on our backs out there on the pier. It wasn't all mushy, though, every now and then, she'd try to sneak in a wish to receive some more of those lilies too. Things were changing for us and we were both realizing how much it was changing us too.

We never saw anything that we could definitely say was the Lady in the Bay. I think, instead of Ikey's story consuming us as it once did, both Claire and I were starting to write our own new story, and we were, more or less, writing Ikey's off as another one of his tall tales. It was definitely appreciated but maybe it was just like the many other of his far-fetched fables that he so lovingly shared with us. They were meant to help us in some way that, so many times, we were just too young to realize. The summer kind of went like that for a while. Ikey was helping my grandfather a little more again, and he spent the rest of his time with Miss Anna. We definitely still ate Miss Anna's Fallopal Flappers, or whatever you call those wonderful, sugary cinnamon biscuit treats every time we were invited to partake, but mostly until Jonas arrived I was just as happy as I could be with it just being Claire and me. Jonas was Miss Anna's nephew, the one she said was coming to the island for a visit.

I expected him to be a pale, skinny kid with a stubby, little, black mustache perched above his lip. I also expected him to be wearing those funny brown or green lederhosen short pants, but that's not what he looked like at all. Although his mother, Miss Anna's sister, was from Germany, his father wasn't, and Jonas was as American as Claire and I. He was a normal-looking kid with brown hair and brown eyes and not even one hair on his lip to be found anywhere. Jonas was a very kind kid too, and it didn't take very long for our little gang to become something that was more like seashells, sand dollars and arrowheads all tied together, just like Pocahontas' necklace. Jonas was originally only going to stay with his aunt for a week, but I guess, just as she did, he liked the place so much that he ended up staying for the rest of the summer. With him being there I once again, realized that there are some people who come into your life who just seem to fit. No matter what age you are or what you've ever been through, somehow, you just know they are, as unexplainable as it may be, a predestined gift from above.

We'd soon learn that Jonas was that for Claire and I, and I know that we were that for him too. Jonas' father died while serving in the military, and I guess things like that make you grow up quicker than most kids his age. With all that occurred in his young life, he seemed to be a little more mature than I thought Claire and I were—well, more than I was anyway. When Ikey saw that all of us got along so well, that old tanned man decided to revisit his Lady in the Bay story, but this time, it was going to be to all three of us. I was glad that he did too. I think Claire and I had, unfortunately, let the curiosity and belief in Ikey's tale wear off, and I kind of missed it, and I'm pretty sure Claire too. Ikey set up his second round of that cherished story in almost the same fashion as he did in the first. He pointed out into the bay and he walked all three of us to the edge of the water. He showed all of the same intensity in his eyes and his theatrics that were just as intriguing as before.

This time, however, he added a few things that he seemed to forget or just decided to leave out of his original version. This time, as he spoke to the three of us, he described a beautiful necklace that was meticulously made by the elders of Pocahontas' tribe—one we never told him that we found. He said it was made from seashells, sand dollars and arrowheads. He described how all of those beautiful elements were so painstakingly strung together with a thick leather band. He also told us how the Lady in the Bay lost her cherished necklace and that she was still looking for it to this day. He also told us that other locals had their own birthright to tell the Lady in Bay's secret story as well. All of this was starting to make more and more sense to Claire and I and it was also getting Jonas as excited about the story as we were the first time we heard it. Since it wasn't our birthright to pass on the story, he asked us to keep his secret as we did before and, once again, I'd feel guilty for not telling my grandmother. After Ikey was finished, he left us all sitting on the beach together.

Claire and I filled Jonas in on some of the things that Ikey didn't know about or at least didn't say. We told Jonas about the necklace that we found and the farewells from the locals that day out on the bay with Conway. Then we told him about everything that we saw at the museum, to include that old, burnt canoe. We also let Jonas know that Ikey's last name was Rolfe. I confidently said, "If anyone knows the real story about the Lady in the Bay, it had to be him." Once we filled Jonas in on everything we knew, he was every bit as captivated by the Lady in the Bay and in finding her as Claire and I ever were. Being more mature than we were, he had what he thought was a more sensible plan about how we could actually accomplish that task though. He felt, instead of hiding anything from Ikey, we should go directly to the source and see if he'd help us. The truth was important to Jonas and hiding something from someone that he cared about was just as bad as a lie to him.

A certain amount of relief came over me because, if we all agreed on Jonas' simple but improved plan, we all knew Ikey could help us as much as anyone could. After all, it was his story. He wasn't a come-here or from anywhere else other than the island. After we introduced Jonas to the undeniable wisdom of Fort Fishing Shack, we once again had all of the necessary checks and hearts in place. This time, with Jonas, more or less, leading the way, we were more motivated in finding the Lady in the Bay than ever before. When we went to Ikey, he seemed to strangely be waiting on us to confess all that we had been doing before Jonas got there. That old man was so odd sometimes, but when we finally told him everything, to include finding what we thought was her necklace, he fiendishly smiled and told us that he knew exactly what to do.

He asked us to hold off on telling our families, though, because he still felt that they should see her for themselves, and Claire's idea of getting a picture of her first was a good way to ensure there wouldn't be any questions about her validity, and that way there wouldn't be any chance of scaring her away either. Ikey reminded us that Pocahontas loved looking for buried treasure as much as she did anything else. Since we found her necklace, he recommended that we put it in a treasure box and bury it at the farthest tip of the island. He further explained how that particular place was one of her most favorite places to play when she was a little girl. I don't know if Ikey realized it or not but the place that he was talking about was another place that we weren't allowed to go by ourselves. I think he thought we'd be inviting him along when we went but that's not quite what we did. To get there, you had to cross a small shallow inlet, but if you didn't pay attention to the tide, it would come in and trap you on the other side until it went back out again. This place was near the hole in the wall fishing spot that Conway showed us from the waterside that day.

I never really disobeyed my grandparents, but I was going to do exactly that once again for something so big and important as burying Pocahontas' treasured necklace in just the right spot. I don't think Ikey ever thought we'd go to the tip of the island on our own but we knew we were going to go there as fast as we could after he told us where the best place to bury such a treasure was. We just didn't want to wait any longer now that finding the Lady in the Bay was so pressing to us once again. Unlike getting up early in the morning to catch Conway before he went out, we broke another rule and snuck out of the house late at night, but this time, it was to bury a treasure, not to catch a bunch of crabs. After checking the tide report the best we knew how, we felt that we knew enough to see that it would still be low tide at the time of our planned departure. If everything went as planned, we'd have plenty of time to bury Pocahontas' treasure and make it home long before anyone, to include Conway, ever got up.

My grandfather had so many of those old, red toolboxes that I knew he wouldn't miss if, somehow, one of them left his inventory. So, with that, we had everything we needed for our trip ready in no time. I even grabbed that same yellow flashlight that we used to see through those DDT mosquito-killing clouds. This time, it was even more effective in guiding our way to the tip of the island than it ever helped us see through those terrible, toxic, black clouds. By the time we got there, I bet we thought we heard something following us in the water ten times or more. We all knew this time we might actually have contact from the historical side for real. Ikey's idea not only included burying the necklace inside of a treasure chest for the Lady in the Bay to find, but he also wanted each one of us to include a letter about the others to let her know why we thought the others that we wrote about were so deserving of such an honor as personally finding her was.

Ikey left strict instructions for us not to let anyone see what we wrote about the others, and he even included his own letters of recommendation for each of us in sealed envelopes for us to include in that old, red toolbox. I don't know about Ikey sometimes, but he said if any of us told the others about what they wrote, it would diminish the integrity of the plan, and, without a doubt, that alone would scare away who we sought out the most. As kids, we didn't really have any idea what he was talking about half of the time but at least he wasn't saying Nipple Tooth anymore, so we followed his directions to a T. Besides, Ikey proved many times that he knew a lot more about the island and the Lady in the Bay than we did, so we listened to him. By this time, and with the help of my fingers, once again, I think I figured out that Ikey was the great, great, great, great, great, grandson of Pocahontas and John Rolfe. Yes, John Rolfe, not John Smith, so he had to be giving us the best advice that anyone could give, or so we thought.

In our reasoning, Ikey's heritage explained his piercing blue eyes on one side and the deep, dark-brownness from the other. It also was our reasoning for how well he seemed to know all of the things that he told us about. As I started writing my letter to include in the treasure chest I wrote about Jonas first; I wrote about how loyal and brave he was. From the second he got to the Island he always had the best plans and made the most sense with them too. I also wrote about how he dreamed about joining the military someday just like his father, and my grandfather, and how courageous I knew he'd be. Letters like this weren't often written by kids our age, and it took some thinking to give them their proper justice. When I wrote my letter about Claire, I didn't think I'd ever stop writing, or at least not until the ink ran out of my pen. I just had so much to say about her. She was the most incredible person I'd ever met. After my third page of writing, which was mostly about how wonderful I thought she was, I lovingly ended her letter with the now-familiar thought.

There are some people who come into your life who just seem to fit, no matter what age you are or what you've ever been through, you just know they are, as unexplainable as it may be, a predestined gift from above. I could have probably just written that last part and left well enough alone, but Claire deserved the best that I could give, so I gave it. I don't know what the others wrote about me but because Ikey said for us to keep it to ourselves, I didn't guess I ever would. I hope, although I broke out of the house in the middle of the night after stealing my grandfather's old red toolbox, and questionably borrowed his flashlight while breaking a fully known curfew, that I was an honest person. I hope they wrote that I lived with forgiveness, courage, empathy and grace, and that I'd always let love lead the way just like a sand dollar. I hoped both Claire and Jonas thought of me as someone who would stand up for his friends and family, no matter what and regardless of the consequences.

I just wanted to be someone they'd never forget, regardless of how old we got or where we ever moved away to. After we reached the tip of the island and having the necklace and private letters safely inside of my grandfather's old toolbox, it didn't take very long to bury it; no more than ten minutes. It did take quite a bit longer to get back home though. All I could think about after we buried our make shift treasure chest was how much trouble I'd be in, especially after being on the tip of the island by ourselves that late at night. I felt that way because being the great nautical minds that we evidently weren't, we—or, should I say, I—had the tide schedule completely backwards and what we thought was the last part of low tide was actually the beginning of high tide. It didn't take hardly any time to bury our treasure where Ikey thought was the best place to bury it but it took even less time for the water to start rushing in and become too high for us to safely pass back over the same way we came in.

We looked for another way out, but it was no use. We were stuck. We all knew it would be at least five or six hours before we'd be able to get back home safely, so there was absolutely nothing else we could do but wait it out. I thought to myself, *this is not good at all*. There was no telling how much explaining I would have to do or what sewer line I was going to have to dig out after this adventure was said and done. Then Jonas, our voice of reason, spoke up, and, after he did a little calculating of his own without needing to use his fingers, he felt pretty confident that we may still be okay with time. We just had to wait and see. His rationale did calm me down a bit and Claire never seemed overly worried, so we dug in and sleuthfully watched what we had just finished burying. As the tide kept crashing in, it was starting to look like the collection of repetitive waves were beginning to dig up our make-shift treasure chest.

It was really dark outside but the flashing glimmers from the moon and stars lit the area in question just enough for us to be able to somewhat see it. It had to because our dying flashlight surely wasn't keeping up with anything on its own. The moonlight also allowed us to see what we all swore was someone reaching towards our once buried treasure chest. Whatever or whoever it was seemed to be pulling that old, red toolbox towards them with each crash of the tides changing waves. Then, all of a sudden, with one big tug, something did jerk what we buried out into the bay. Almost immediately that old, red toolbox was completely out of sight. This time, we knew for a fact that our plan was working. This happened almost exactly as Ikey said it would, and all three of us saw it with our own eyes. As we youthfully reasoned the Lady in the Bay just got her necklace back and, after she read all of our letters, she'd probably even want to come over for dinner with all of our families without a doubt. She'd see that we were all worthy enough to share her not only with each other but also with the ones who we loved the most—our families.

I don't know if we expected that to happen right then and there or in a few hours, but it didn't happen quite as we may have thought it would. I can remember thinking, *maybe she's slow like me, and our letters may have had to simmer with her for a while, or maybe she wanted to wait for the perfect time to reveal herself and we'd just have to wait it out once again.* I simply didn't know but we all felt sure that we saw her take the toolbox and now something had to happen, it just had to. At the very least, we all knew this time we made contact with her, and that's further than we'd ever gotten before. We got a little wet wading our way away from the tip of the Island when a safe enough time came to pass back over, but it wasn't too bad. We didn't miss Conway or Pogo on the way home though. I don't know why I thought this was a good idea but, instead of letting Jonas decide what we should do next, once Conway saw us, I pretended like we were there again that early in the morning to go out crabbing with him once more.

That's the thing about a lie: once you tell one, the additional lies you have to tell to cover up the first one always comes back to bite you. In this case, it could mean literally. If there was any good to come out of my deception it was that Jonas got a chance to see all of the things from the waterside that Claire and I got to see on our last early morning trip out in the bay with the Crab Man. This time, however, and, unfortunately for us all, we didn't have any of those savory Fallopian Flippers, or whatever you call those wonderful, sugary cinnamon biscuit treats of Miss Anna's with us, and Pogo's humpty dumpty self was very much as awake and flirtatious as he'd ever been. That alone would have been punishment enough for anything we may have done because this trip simply wasn't as enjoyable as the last. Jonas did get to see a different view of the Island, but even he got growled at and humped on quite a bit during this trip out. When I got home, I didn't lie, but I didn't tell the complete truth either. I told my grandmother that Claire, Jonas and I went crabbing with Conway and that dumb dog Pogo again.

It may not have been a total lie, but I knew as well as I knew my name was henry, it wasn't the complete truth either. As I finally got to go to sleep, this time, I once again realized that I never hid anything from my grandmother before all of this started and now it seems like was doing that all the time now. I slept a long time after I got home but it wasn't a peaceful sleep. I guess my conscious knew all of the real truths, even though the rest of me seemed to be straying pretty far away from them. I guess that lingering guilty feeling made me want to tell Ikey everything that happened first about our trip to the tip of the island when we saw him the next day. I wanted to see what his reaction or guidance might be after we, unquestionably, saw the Lady in the Bay take the treasure chest toolbox out into the bay. I tried to get him to listen, I really did; we all did, but, like I said, smitten is smitten no matter how old you are.

Evidently, old Ikey was a little more than smitten too. Miss Anna and Ikey had become so close in such a short amount of time that, without us kids knowing anything about it, they decided to get married, and they didn't want to wait to do it either. He asked her, I'm guessing, when we were out with Conway, and they used every minute after to start planning their wedding for a quick two weeks later. That old man never ceased to amaze anyone, especially me, but, jokingly, I thought I sure hoped he didn't agree to any nuptials just so he could have some of Miss Anna's Farfignugens, or whatever you call those delicious, sugary cinnamon biscuit treats whenever he wanted them. The one way I absolutely knew Ikey was honestly getting more serious about Miss Anna was because he recently developed a rather comical health issue. It was kind of an anxious tick that just recently seemed to flare up or, should I say, flare out whenever he saw her or even talked about her. For some unknown reason, if Ikey got a little overly excited about anything that had to do with Miss Anna, that old man would blow a little wind, or flatulence, as some call it out.

I guess it was an unpleasant reminder that he was nervous about something. To a bunch of kids, there aren't too many things that are much funnier than a good ol' unexpected gastrointestinal release from an old, tan man. However, to Ikey, understandably, it was much more than a little embarrassing. It was even more embarrassing than the pink culottes were after his juicy tobacco bath. He took beano and even had some kind of strong prescription gas medicine, but nothing seemed to help him. Now, with his wedding coming up so quickly, he knew full well that occasion was probably going to be as nerve-racking as it gets, and he felt pretty sure that his body was going to let him and everyone else know about it too. We should have known something was going on because, over the past few weeks, whenever he'd talk about Miss Anna, the cheese would inadvertently slice its way out into to the public.

Each time it happened, he'd turn that shade of red that was most commonly attributed to Conway instead of himself. With us kids so often in his audience, we would try not to laugh, but we couldn't help ourselves. We were kids; what would you expect us to do when someone farts all over themselves out of nowhere? On Ikey's big day, he wanted to say the "I do's" at the end of the pier where the probability of the sound from a different kind of wind would at least have a chance to drown out anything his body might make. If that was his reasoning for a selection of location, I thought that was a pretty good idea, I had to admit. When his special day came, he once again cleaned up like a new penny, and although he was always happy, I'd never seen him as happy as he was that day. My grandfather, Jonas and myself were all groomsman. Claire, my grandmother and Claire's mother were Miss Anna's bridesmaids. Watching Claire walk down the pier almost gave me a bubble in my own stomach, but I had discipline and I held off. As everyone in the wedding party went to the end of the pier, the others watching gathered around on each side of the couple farther down the pier.

Ikey's expected nervousness seemed to have subsided, and I was happy for him in one way, and in another I was a little childishly disappointed. I was kind of looking forward to a "buttocksinal" concert from that old man but it didn't happen. I didn't understand how Ikey could have healed himself so quickly, but my grandfather seemed to know. That big man evidentially shared some of his knowledge on the subject with his old tanned friend earlier that day, and his guidance worked too. In the early years of the restaurant, my grandfather couldn't leave the cooking line for hours on end, and, sometimes, as he said, the pressure would build-up, if you know what I mean. To save himself from being embarrassed or grossing the customers out, he took a paper to-go bag out and made as much noise opening it up as he could. That was all the cover-up that anyone would need, and, even though Ikey couldn't very well have a paper bag up there with him in front of everyone at the end of the pier, he could and did have a paper heart as the perfect prop to crinkle on for the same effect if needed.

I knew my grandfather could improvise anything into working, and the knowledge that he passed on to Ikey worked so well that Ikey never had that particular problem again. Thinking back to the first time we met Ikey in front of Scrooch's, I'm so glad that I got to see what my grandfather saw in him. He was simply a lonely man who needed a family. We were still that for him but now we all were getting another very special family member, and it wasn't just because of her delicious, sugary cinnamon biscuit treats either. Miss Anna was the icing on top for all of us but, more so, she was just what Ikey needed. For each of them, there was that realization that everyone at their wedding saw first-hand. The realization was there are some people who come into your life who just seem to fit. No matter what age you are or what you've ever been through, you just know they are, as unexplainable as it may be, a predestined gift from above. Miss Anna was that for Ikey, and I know that Ikey was that for her too.

M. A. COLE

# EAGLE FEATHERS

The summer and all the time that I got to spend with my grandparents and my friends was quickly coming to an end. Jonas was going back home soon, and I was going to be back at school in Richmond not too long after. When I thought about being so far away from Claire, my heart hurt, but, in reality, it really wasn't really that far at all. I know it was puppy love, but it was real love for us nonetheless. She was the first girl I ever had a second thought about, and, by then, almost all of my thoughts involved her in some way. As we quickly aged throughout the summer, we still remembered the Lady in the Bay and our mission to find her but, once again, it didn't seem as pressing as Jonas and my leaving was. We were the three musketeers who often acted more like the three stooges, but it was fun. It was more than fun; it was family. Like I've said throughout my whole life, when my grandfather built something, the people around weren't just customers and they weren't just friends either; they were family from the beginning. Claire and Jonas would always be my family. Our paths, as it happens in families sometimes, seem to be going in different directions, but we'll always be a family from here on out.

Jonas was the first to leave. The morning he was set to go, Claire and I met him at Miss Anna's—who I guess we should be calling Mrs. Anna now—but Claire had taken a picture of Jonas and we glued it on a poster of a military general to show our respect for what we knew he would be someday. We also knew that we'd all stay in touch by phone and through letters, but it's not the same as being together in person, and we all knew it. As Jonas was leaving, that sensible boy had some very foreknowing tears in his eyes. I guess since he was more mature than we were, he knew somehow that he'd never see that beautiful Island again, and, unfortunately, time would prove his tears to be true. On the morning that I left, it was a little different. I knew that I'd be back down to the campground just about every weekend. I wouldn't be there all the time like I had been that summer, but I'd still be back pretty often.

It was sad that I was leaving too, but not like it was with Jonas. Besides, on my trips back, I could bring some barbecue back down with me. We could have crab cakes from the Hole in the Wall on Saturdays and barbecue from Hank's on Sundays. We might not have anything else planned out, but our culinary choices sounded like they should be set in stone. Claire had school herself, so by the time the weekends came around, we really didn't feel like we missed out on much after all. As the next few years went by, Claire and I became more serious about each other than we probably should have at our age. It seemed alright, though, because we were already family in our youthful way of thinking. In my senior year of high school, my grandfather shocked everyone by telling us he was thinking about selling the campground. None of us wanted him to actually go through with it, but he was getting quite a bit older himself and we understood that he had worked and improvised enough for three lifetimes. If you judge a man's life by how he provided for his family, my grandfather was as successful as any man that ever lived.

His provisions weren't necessarily always in material means but in regard to love, forgiveness, courage, empathy and grace, I couldn't imagine a better teacher. He evidentially had a few sand dollars on the farm in North Carolina where he grew up too. He always gave credit to his values from his time spent in the military. I think that's why he and Jonas hit it off so well. On many of our ride-a-longs on the bulldozer, he'd tell me how he wished that I'd join the military after I graduated from high school. He felt that would be the perfect beginning for a young man, or even a young family starting out. I don't know what it was about him and Ikey winking at me, but he and Ikey would both wink when they said things that they hoped would stick in my mind. My grandfather knew how I felt about Claire and how long I felt that way. Everyone expected us to be together forever, even her parents.

They all seemed to feel like they already knew what our combined futures had in store for us. Jonas even saw it early on and never once thought any differently. With graduation right around the corner, whether we wanted to or not, Claire and I would be adults, or at least a little more adult-ish soon. She wanted to go to college to become a teacher. I actually could see that with all the patience she had with me over the years, but I had no idea what I was going to do. Jonas was going to live out his dreams and would soon be heading off to the military, and, once again, he'd be leaving first. Ikey was the only one throughout the years who seemed to be aging backwards. Every time Claire and I saw him, he looked more like the good years of Benjamin Buttons than he did anything else. He didn't look like that old cigar store Indian anymore at all. Married life and Mrs. Anna's Fuzzle Flompers, or whatever you call those delicious, sugary cinnamon biscuit treats, must have been treating him well. I'm was so happy for my old friend; he deserves all the beautiful things that life can bring.

Ikey would still ask both Claire and I if we saw the Lady in the Bay from time to time and he'd wink at us right after he did. That man was so special to our childhood. It's a little different now than when we were little kids, but that's the way life is—it constantly changes and forces you to change with it. It doesn't matter who you are or what you're doing because, when life decides to force a change, life always wins, no matter how hard anyone fights against it. My grandfather finally decided to make a big change for himself too. He called his own bluff and sold the campground the month before I graduated from high school. I thought he and my grandmother would move back to Richmond after he sold it but, as usual, I was wrong. He bought a house on the road down the street from the campground instead. It was just as close to Claire's parents' house as the campground was. He may not have had to work as hard as he once did, but he also didn't want to leave the island that he grew to love so much either.

They only lived in that house for a month before we found out that my grandmother was sick. She had cancer, and, although she knew something was wrong for a long time, she never would tell anyone because, as she put it, there was simply too much work to do. She was always more concerned about taking care of the rest of us than she ever was about herself. If grace means receiving a gift that you don't deserve, then my grandmother was the most selfless and graceful person I've ever been blessed enough to know. She died a short time after she found out just how sick she was. I've often wondered if she'd still be alive if some doctor didn't tell her how sick they thought she was, but I guess no one will ever know. That kind of news gets in your mind and, sometimes, it's as life-threatening as any disease ever will be. Either way, my family lost its matriarch, and my grandfather lost his true reason for living.

We all tried to change the way he felt but he just didn't want to live without her. He died almost two months to the day after my grandmother passed. The doctor said that he died from heart failure. That's one doctor I don't think I could have agreed with more. His heart would have always failed without her. That's what that kind of love does. There our family was, a kingdom, of sorts, without a king or queen to lovingly lead the way. For me, my grandparents, as odd as it might be to hear, were two of the best friends I ever had, and now they're gone, and they're gone forever too. I hadn't spent as much time with them as I did when I was younger. I guess I thought they'd always be there, but they weren't. This still gives me some of the greatest regret that my heart has ever felt. With both of my grandparents gone so suddenly, I kept thinking back to my grandfather's wishes for how he wanted me to start out my own adult life. For him, his greatest desire for me was to go into the military. The military was where he started and where he learned the lessons that he credited for his journey out of poverty and into manhood as he so often put it.

I hurt so bad from the loss of my grandparents that my grandfather's desires for my future all but consumed me. I never mentioned them to Claire or my parents or really anyone else for that matter. Claire did help in other ways though. She was there for me as much as I'd let anyone be at the time. One night, a few days after my grandfather's funeral, for some reason, the letters that Ikey asked us to write about each came to the forefront of my thoughts. I still remembered what I hoped Claire, Jonas and even Ikey wrote about me. I hoped they all wrote that I was someone who would always stand up for his friends and family no matter what the consequences were. Reflecting back to the wishes that I had for myself as young boy and knowing full well what my grandfather's wishes for me were, I started to realize that was what I wanted for myself also.

If he gave credit to the military for making him the man he was, then I don't believe I could find a better path for myself. Besides, the military option came with the highest recommendation possible—it came from someone I respected and loved as much as anyone, my grandfather. Whether I was correct in my way of thinking or not, I honestly believed, after all that just happened to my family, if I chose anything else, it would have been against everything those wonderful and loving people ever taught me. If they were still here, I know they would have supported me with anything I did, but they're not anymore, so I felt I had to support their wishes for the start of my adult life. I knew they'd never lead me astray, so without any more thought or consideration about anything else, I called Jonas to see what I needed to do to join up. I should have talked this over with Claire. I know I should have, but my pain was so great from the loss of both of my grandparents that I didn't want anyone to try and talk me out of what I felt I needed to do to honor their memory, not even Claire. I truly felt it was the very least I could do.

I loved Claire and I didn't want to lose her, but I had to do what I had to do, as selfish as that may sound. Jonas was scheduled to report to basic training in the upcoming week. We had no idea that, after he contacted his recruiter they'd allow me to go with him under the buddy system. I just had to get a physical, enlist and agree to leave when he did. As soon as I heard the news from Jonas, I scheduled my physical and enlistment appointment on the next available time slot, which happened to be the very next day. After all the swearing-in was done, I immediately told my parents, then I had to tell Claire what I had done. I didn't feel that I was joining the military for myself; I didn't really think I was joining for Claire either, even though I hoped that was partly true, even if a little rushed. I think, when it comes down to it, I joined the military to grant the last wishes that my grandparents had for me.

After I spoke with Claire, it was glaringly obvious she just couldn't understand why I felt I had to leave. We both knew, regardless of how close we'd always been, we weren't ready to get married, at least not yet. I hoped we could figure things out, even if for a while it had to be from a place that was a little farther away than either of us ever expected it to be. Claire was heartbroken though. In a strange way, I'm glad I didn't talk to her about my decision first because, if I would have known how bad this was going to affect her, I don't know if I could have gone through with it, but it was too late either way. I never meant to hurt her, but I still had to do this for my grandparents. I knew she didn't mean it, but, on our last day together she told me that she couldn't come to the airport to see me off. She said she didn't think she'd ever stop crying if she did. To be truthful, I didn't know where we were actually leaving things, but she kept her word and didn't come to the airport on the day I left. My parents, Ikey, Mrs. Anna and a few other relatives and friends came, but not Claire. Her not being there tore me up inside but I still felt that I was doing the right thing.

If I ever thought growing up was confusing, it was nothing compared to this young adulthood mess, I thought. Ikey, as he did so often in my youth, pulled me aside and gave me a little comforting speech. My old, tanned buddy told me how proud my grandparents would be of me and how proud he was as well. Ikey's kind words did make me feel a little better, but my heart was still crushing over how I left things with Claire. Ikey also gathered Jonas and I together before we got on the plane and he gave us both an eagle feather. He said it was one of the highest honors that he could give because it represented courage, one of his ancestors' key virtues to live by. He then gave us a final wink and once again told us if we ever needed help not to forget about the Lady in the Bay. Jonas and I laughed and thought, *that crazy old man never gives up, does he?* Besides, in truth, we already knew after training we were going to be headed to the Middle East.

I doubt very seriously we'd ever find a fictitious character from our past there, especially since we never found her where she was supposed to be. I don't even think that place has a bay for any Pocahontas lady to be in anyway. From what I was told, there is just a bunch of sand, but instead of being on a beach, this sand was in a desert that stretched out as far as the eye could see. This sand was said to be full of landmines instead of seashells, sand dollars or arrowheads. Training went well for both Jonas and I. I wrote to my family and I wrote to Claire too. At least my family wrote me back after I did. I could feel that I broke something with Claire that I never thought could be broken and now I was suffering the consequences that I'm sure I very much deserved. Once a little more light was shed on the severity of where I was going and what I'd soon be doing, I began to realize what the constant agony that I felt over Claire was doing to me, and what it could possibly do to others too. I had to find a way to get a handle on my emotions, at least a little more than I had been because, if I didn't, someone else might have to pay for my pain.

In the military, mistakes are so often paid with someone else's life and someone else's life was more than I was willing to risk just because I couldn't handle my own feelings. It was so hard, but I had to make myself compartmentalize all of the pain that I had for my grandparents and Claire the best I could. Once I realized this and tried my hardest to bury what I could. Those emotions still seeped out at times, but they didn't have complete control over me as they once did. The thing about hiding your emotions is, although the stabbing pain may subside, a certain kind of numbness comes in and takes its place. That numbness began to prevent me from caring about some of the things that I probably should have cared about more, to include myself.

I'm not sure which emotion was worse, but I figured at least that numbness could come in handy in the desert. My efforts of compartmentalization consisted of remembering all of the beautiful times I had in my youth, especially with Claire, but I had to also accept what we were now. Now we seemed to be just another young love gone awry as most do. In a short amount of time, I realized that my grandfather was right when he said that the military would change you. I was definitely beginning to change. I just didn't know if it was for the better or not. I still thought about Claire every day, but I couldn't blame her for anything anymore. It was my decision to leave the way I did, and I had to live with the consequences. While working on that, I realized that, unlike Ikey, the military doesn't fabricate things... well, not about sending their people to a war in the desert anyway. To be completely honest, there were times that I thought maybe I was finally getting what I deserved. Maybe I deserved to be punished in a sense for not spending more time with my grandparents at the end of their lives. Maybe I needed to be punished for ruining my relationship with Claire. That was a relationship that was supposed to last a lifetime, I simply didn't know.

Jonas felt a little differently about going to the war than I did. He was proud and he even seemed excited, but I, for the most part, was still numb to the fact. He was going to honor his father's memory like I still hoped I would do for my grandparents, but we were still thinking about this whole situation completely different. Unfortunately, even though his bravery and our specific goals never changed, after our first skirmish, I think even his eyes were opened to exactly how evil war really is. On most of our missions, we were sent out in teams of four. There was Jonas and I, then Chappy, our sergeant, and lastly, Cash, another young soldier who was crazier than anyone that was ever allowed to carry a gun should be. Cash was a short, muscular guy from Bakersfield, California. He was a black belt in something, and he wanted everyone to know it too. I didn't see what the big deal was because, hell, we had M-16s. I'll take a machine gun over the ability to perform a roundhouse kick any day.

He was a good guy though, but he was cocky, and he seemed to have that same problem that Ikey had before my grandfather set him straight with the paper heart trick before his wedding. Cash's wind issues were obviously more purposeful than Ikey's. I guess he was trying to be funny or release a little pressure of his own, but he was already more jagged than the rest of us were. I'm sure that was because this was his second tour and we knew he had already seen quite a bit. He was the only one of us who had any kind of combat experience, so, whether we had to smell him or not, we definitely listened to what he had to say. Sargent Chapman, Chappy as we called him was a big ole', brown-headed country boy from Valdosta, Georgia. He was in charge but, regardless of his rank, he transferred in from a desk job, so he didn't have a clue of what he was doing at first either. He didn't seem to have the temperament for the military. He was almost overly calm and peaceful, and almost nothing rattled his cage.

He was a smart guy but sometimes I felt like we had to remind him that we were actually in a war and not back at home fishing in the crick. Our four-man crew's daily mission most often consisted of clearing out anything that was in shooting distance of this group of roads in the various supply lines to other units in the theatre. Some days it didn't seem like the constant crackle from the M-16s and whatever kind of gun the so-called enemy had would ever stop ringing out. On other days, we barely heard a single pop or anything else out of anyone. Every day for almost a year out of our two-year tour, we would go out and check on our assigned area and, no matter whether we had to crackle or pop or even wait to do either, we all began to become more than a little proficient at what we were assigned to do. Each member of our little group had a specific job that, quite frankly, we eventually became quite good at.  Cash always volunteered to be the point man, which meant that fool actually looked forward to walking out in the open to try and stir up trouble if there was any around to be found. If he didn't have a death wish, he sure as hell acted like he did most of the time.

Jonas, because of how well he did in training, was our lookout, which was basically the sniper of the group. I always knew he was more patient and mature than anyone I'd ever known, so he was proving it with his assigned role. He'd have to wait motionless for three or four hours or more at times.  He not only covered the rest of us, but he'd often have to travel back to camp alone on many of our outings and being alone in the military is never a good thing. He'd get stuck by himself sometimes because he'd have to set up so far away to be able to see everything, especially all of us all at once. Chappy still had a desk job in a sense, at least we joked with him about that as our radioman. His job was probably the most important out of all of ours, but we jokingly let him know he was still doing the job of an office worker. He'd call in coordinates and notify everyone about what was going on wherever we were.

My job sounds horrible, but it really wasn't. I was what they called a thumper. A thumper is basically a munitions man. There were really two sides to my job—one being to try and find all the landmines that I could and blow them up. The other side of what I did was to set out our own in the paths of where we thought the bad guys would be coming from. I think with my job we missed a recycling opportunity, but I never said anything about that; I just did what I was told to do. As the military does, the better we got at what we did, the more they kept assigning more and more things for us to do, and with every new assignment there was also an ever-growing danger that, unfortunately, came along with it. That crazy Cash would always lead the way and rarely take cover when he really needed to. His overconfident acts were really selfless because he'd always seem to take the immediate pressure off of the rest of us and he probably did that while gassing up the place too.

He was, more or less, a self-nominated decoy while the rest of us completed our parts of the mission. Jonas wasn't too far behind in the bravery department, if at all. I knew he wouldn't be either. He was definitely smarter and more rightfully cautious than Cash though. Being over there together made Jonas and I—and really, all four of us— become as much like brothers as any brothers ever were, regardless of our numerous differences. When things were calm, Jonas and I would often tell Chappy and Cash some of the stories from that adventurous summer in our shared past. Of course, I told them about Claire, my parents and grandparents. Jonas often told them about his parents and his aunt and her delicious Fajita Fidgets, or whatever you call those wonderful, sugary cinnamon biscuit treats. We both talked about how Ikey made that summer so much fun by creating a story about someone he named the Lady in the Bay and how he seemingly had the whole island involved in one way or another with the possibility of us actually finding that fictitious historical figure.

We also told them about how we buried that old, red tool box at the tip of the Island with the necklace and letters inside, and how we actually would have sworn that we all saw Pocahontas herself pull that makeshift treasure chest out into the bay. When we told the other two about that, Cash blurted out, "And you think I'm the crazy one." We even told the other guys about the Indian names Ikey gave us during one of our many evenings with him on the beach. Ikey named Jonas Taka Anwa, which, according to our old, blue-eyed, Indian guide, meant "shooting star." I was Mawi Hewa and Claire was Ekiwa Hewa. Our elderly matchmaker was always at work back then, as my Indian name meant "right heart" and Claire's "left heart." Those stories still hurt a little when I think back to them for several reasons, but I was just glad that old man didn't rename me Nipple Tooth, I guess. As a gift, Jonas and I gave Cash and Chappy their own tribal names for at least pretending like they were interested in our reflections back to such a wonderful time our lives. In truth, even though Ikey taught us a few native words, Cash and Chappy would never know if they were actual translations or not, so we may have taken a few liberties with naming our friends, but we tried.

We named Chappy Wassa Himata, which we told him meant "peaceful big brother." He wasn't but a few years older than we were, but the way he looked out after us is why both Jonas and I felt his Indian name definitely fit, no matter if it was fully legitimate or not. For us, it was a term of endearment, and he seemed to greatly appreciate it. When it came to Cash, his name probably even suited him better than any of the rest of ours. We bestowed upon Cash the honorable and legendary Indian name of Mutta Suka. For the most part, Jonas and I held our chuckles in while we were contemplating what we were going to name that psychopath, but it wasn't easy. Mutta Suka, from what we knew, somewhat translated into the words devil skunk.

He was always so pumped up out in front of everyone during our missions that he really did remind us all of the Tasmanian devil. He also had so many of those other skunk-like qualities that his Native American name was almost too perfect. I wanted to tell him about my grandfather's paper bag trick, but I didn't think he would have cared or followed suit, so I just let the Mutta Suka be what a Mutta Suka was going to be. Completely literal or not, the guys were extremely appreciative of their new Indian warrior names as we described them. Cash even wrote his Indian name on a piece of masking tape and put it across his actual name tag on his uniform. I guess, from that point, he wanted everyone to know that he really was a Mutta Suka. Chappy didn't do that, but we all knew that he never took his role as our big brother lightly. That man looked out for his little brothers in every way a big brother can, and he took such pride in doing so.

With these guys, I once again realized that there are some people who come into your life who just seem to fit, no matter what age you are, or what you've ever been through; you just know they are, as unexplainable as it may be, a predestined gift from above. Cash and Chappy were that for Jonas and I, and I knew we were always that for them too. Jonas and I talked about Ikey so much that Cash asked what his Indian name was. Ikey never really told us, and I guess none of us were ever smart enough to ask him back then, but, jokingly, I replied by saying, "If I'd be naming him, I'd name him Chief Fulla Bulla." The guys laughed, and I truly didn't mean any disrespect towards Ikey because I love the man, but he is the only person I have ever heard of who faked a birthday just to eat some treats, even if those treats did include fruitcake and Mrs. Anna's Funogamy Fritters, or whatever you called those delicious, sugary cinnamon biscuit things. Sometimes, after our missions, Jonas and I would kind of separate from the others for a while.

We'd talk about home and our parents, and, of course, I'd always seem to bring up Claire. Jonas would supportively listen to me about something I thought I'd be over by now, but to be truthful, I don't think I'll ever fully get over losing that girl. Her bluest of blue eyes still haunted me at times. I think what gets me the most is I can almost understand her not being at the airport when I left. Mainly because it was so sudden and she was so upset, but I've written to her hundreds of times and not once did she ever write me back—not even a single response. Calling isn't an option from where we are, and I don't see it being one until we're out of here either. I'd like to be able to think about her less, but I can't. When I'd shut up about Claire long enough for Jonas to share his thoughts, for some reason he would always get on the subject of dying. His dad's death would always live with him as my grandparents' would for me, so I knew very well what he was talking about, but unlike him, I wasn't as supportive about that subject as he was.

He wasn't scared of death; it was quite the opposite. He almost had an infatuation with it. The song, "Who Do You Love" by George Thorogood, was out at the time, and one of the lines was, "I'm just twenty-two and I don't mind dying." Jonas must have taken that song and those lyrics to heart because, even though we weren't twenty-two yet, he'd always end our talks by referencing that song and telling me how, if it was his time to go, he didn't mind going. I did my best to try and change the way he thought, or at least get him to stop talking about death, but he never would. I had already lost so many people that I cared about and we had death all around us now, so I just didn't want to hear any talk like that anymore. I guess I thought talking about it, in some weird way, might increase the odds of it actually happening more often. At times, I'd even try to preach to him. I'd start by trying to remember and pass on some of the lessons I learned from church as a boy, but he'd always outsmart me with my own medicine. He knew more than what I was attempting to do, so I stopped.

# ALWAYS GUILTY

**J**onas just had a knowing about so many things. He knew he'd never see that majestic little Island again, and, evidentially, he knew what was getting ready to happen to all of us very soon somehow too. It's never about you in war; it's always about helping those around you get through it. I know, in our own way, that's what Jonas and I were trying to do for each other. Thinking back, I wish I remembered to tell another one of Ikey's stories, not that it would have changed anything, but I still wish I would have. Again, I have no idea how much of this was true or not, but Ikey told me about the Battle of Cricket Hill several times throughout my youth. He said it was a David and Goliath sort of tale. It was a time where the Gwynn's Island and Mathews County locals and others who were stationed in the area banded together to fight off the mighty British during the War for Independence. They were greatly outnumbered but somehow persevered.

The reason this was so significant to Ikey and the reason he wanted to pass it on to me was that he wanted me to understand that, even if all of the odds seem impossibly stacked against you, there is always hope and, sometimes, even victory in the seemingly impossible. We didn't even get a chance to persevere that day. We didn't even get to where we had planned to start our mission from either. Instead, we ran over a roadside bomb on the way. It was the kind I was supposed to know about and diffuse or even blow up, but that didn't happen. Everyone knows you can't get all those damn things because they're constantly being put down and there were simply too many of them, but I don't know why God didn't see it fit for me to find that one on that terrible day. Cash was ejected from the passenger's seat and Jonas and I had the same fate from the back. Chappy, who was driving, barely had a scratch on him. He unstrapped himself and got out of that mangled Humvee as quickly as he could. He came over to me first, I guess because I was the closest to him.

I don't know if I had a concussion or what was happening, but I felt like I was floating away. I stayed that way for only a few minutes, but it felt like an eternity. They say when you're dying, you see your life flash before your eyes. Since that didn't happen, I could only conclude that I had to force myself to snap out of it and go see if the others needed help. When I got up, Chappy had already made his way over to Cash. Chappy just stood there looking down in what I can only describe as a horrific trance. I knew then Cash was gone then. I then frantically started searching for Jonas and I found him too. He was about fifteen yards from where we were thrown, but in the opposite direction. With all that crimson-red blood splattered all over him, I couldn't think of anything else to do but pull out the eagle feather that Ikey gave me at the airport before we left. Jonas always had his with him too, so I found his in his back pocket and I put a feather in each of my brave brother's hands. I desperately wanted him to know just how courageous I thought he was, even though I knew I wouldn't have much time to do it.

I was almost mad at him at first, but I knew not even he wanted to die that way. He might not have minded dying, but I minded so much for him; he was my brother. The last thing he said to me was, "Henry, I see the star, I see the star... I see home," and then he winked at me as Ikey or my grandfather would have done, and that was it. The tight grip he once had on both eagle feathers loosened and he was gone too. Before I had any time at all to process what had just happened, Chappy, who was still standing over Cash' body looked over at me to confirm what we both already knew. Then, as indescribably painful as it is to say, it was so much worse watching as Chappy put the end of his own rifle in his mouth and pull the trigger. All of a sudden, I had terror chills jolting throughout my body worse than any electrical shock could ever be. I screamed and tripped and fell at least two or three times trying to get over to him, but it was no use. Chappy, our precious, peaceful big brother was gone too.

He left in a completely different horrifying way but it still had the same heartbreaking result. He took his job of taking care of his little brothers seriously, and I guess he couldn't live with the feeling that he didn't do that, even though there wasn't anything at all he could have done to prevent what happened that day. As the medical unit started rushing in a few minutes later, they grabbed me and threw me in the back of another Humvee. It was more like getting arrested than it was like being helped out, but I really didn't care. I don't think I could have ever done what Chappy did, just because I don't know that I could ever be brave enough—if that's bravery. I guess the military thought I might, though, because they flew me and seven others who experienced a similar fate out and back to the states that night on a medical jet. Originally we had over fifty people in that unit, but that day was a massacre, and only seven of us other than the medical support unit were left.

None of this felt real. It was more like having a leading role in a horror movie. The kind where you know you're the main character, the one that never dies, but the one that also knows everyone around you does. That's exactly what happened except for a select cursed few of us. When all of the rushing around stopped, my heart more than realized this part of my life wasn't a movie at all—it was so much worse. Cash, Jonas and Chappy were gone, and they were gone forever too. I never felt life was unfair before then, but now I do. Every negative occurrence that happened in my life up to that point happened in response to something I did wrong or when I didn't plan things out well enough. My grandparents dying hurt a great deal, but they had such a wonderful life and gave so much of themselves that I knew and learned with time that their death was their natural and blessed next move to an even better mansion. This, however, was just too much. I was always taught that if you had a problem, you just work your way through it. You even improvise if you need to.

This was just too big for me to even begin to know how to work through. I guess sometimes your only choices are to either be the mosquito or the bug killer. The problem is, both of those job descriptions suck, and I honestly felt that I lost no matter which one I chose. I was in a bad place and I didn't come close to feeling like I deserved to still be here without the others. That damn numbness that came to visit me so quickly after that had soulless eyes and a razor-sharp sickle. For most of my life I've been somewhat faithful, regardless of the situation. This time I still couldn't blame God for what happened because I didn't feel like he cared enough about us to be there at all. My efforts of compartmentalization this time concluded that, no matter if it was Claire or God, if they didn't care about me, I wasn't going to care about them either. Chappy may have had it right in what he did. I don't know, but, as terrible as it is, that's what that kind of love also does sometimes.

War and all of its evil scrapes off something inside of you that never heals. These guys weren't just my friends; they were my family, and to be truthful, I don't believe I ever want these scars to heal. I could have sworn I had a heart at one time; I thought it was a big one too, but that was before. Now I don't know what I have or what I am. I was in the hospital after that even though I didn't have anything physically wrong with me other than some scrapes, bruises and a little dizziness. A week went by and I started getting restless being a prisoner and knowing full well there was always a military policeman outside my door. Nobody ever came in to do anything with me other than give me three meals a day. I guess someone somewhere was waiting to see what I was going to do next if anything. If anyone says the United States military plays fair, they're lying because the first visitors I did receive a week later were my parents. When I first saw them walk in, I turned away in shame. My mother wasn't having any of that though.

She immediately barked out, "Look at me, boy," and she screamed it even better and louder than any drill instructor ever could. When I looked up at my mother and then my father, I started crying like a little baby. By this time, Cash wasn't the only one who had become a little more than jagged, but none of that mattered with them. I guess that's what that kind of love does also. That was the first time since that day that I spoke about anything, especially about the horror that I was still saturated in. Unlike when I was a child sneaking out of the house to go on whatever adventure, this time, I didn't hide or hold back anything from them; I told them everything. I didn't want to put all that on them, but I felt if I didn't at least try to get it out, my insides were going to rot from coming face to face with those soulless eyes of pure evil. I knew my parents were all I had left then. There were no grandparents, no Jonas, no Chappy, no Cash, no Claire and no God. I didn't forget about Ikey, but he had to be so old by now, I'd be surprised if he was still alive, so probably no Ikey either.

I know it sounds selfish, but I can't take anything else right now. I'm not just living with ghosts; I'm balancing on a tiny single thread of existence here. Neither my mother nor my father left my side for the additional two weeks they made me stay in the hospital. It was like we were all camping in that damn horror movie but, ironically enough, I think I had to do that for the movie to end—if it ever would. I've only heard this happen a few times before but, after that, the military felt that I'd had enough, even with a year to go on my enlistment. They still gave me an honorable discharge and a bunch of fake medals that I didn't deserve. The sergeant who was appointed to me said that I would still be on inactive reserve, which meant they could call me back in at any time, but we both knew that wasn't going to happen. I knew by then they thought I was damaged goods, and I thought it too.

I thought back to the real heroes in World War I, World War II, Korea and most definitely Vietnam. Those guys deserved a get-out-of-hell card much more than I did. Many of those guys saw ten times what I did but, for some reason, deserving or not, in today's military that's what they gave me and the other handful of guys who made it through that day. I went to stay with my parents after that. I would have done that anyway because I didn't have anywhere else to go. When I first got there, for weeks after, I didn't do much but think about all I lost. At night, I'd get on the top of my parents' roof and just stare up at the stars. It was just like Claire and I used to do from the pier on the campground. I didn't have any outcome in mind, I was just looking for a little relief or even guidance that I hoped the stars would provide. I guess that was similar to how I believed they would when I was younger. I'd even see what I thought was a shooting star now and then. I wondered and even hoped that Ikey named Jonas correctly and those stars were our Taka Anwa's way of telling me that he really did make it home.

I began receiving phone calls for the first time in a long time. Ikey called several times but I just couldn't talk to him yet. I loved the man and I was grateful he was still alive and for all he'd done for me throughout my life, but I just couldn't hear any stories about how everything was going to be okay. Surprisingly enough, Claire called too, but for me, it was just too little too late, and besides, I had already categorized her. Sitting on my parents' roof, I think I thought about everything that ever happened in my life and I honestly believe I remembered everything. Most of my life had been truly wonderful, then in a flash, it changed. I knew it wasn't so wonderful then. I don't think I was feeling sorry for myself; I just didn't care about much anymore. Almost all I knew was gone, and if I'd call my life a river, it wasn't flowing at all. Instead, it was a stagnant, stinking cesspool for at least another three or four months after I got home.

I knew it was killing my parents to see me that way and I didn't know how to change it, but my Dad did. One day, my father just got fed up I guess, and he gave me a little project of his own to do. He knew with all of the little projects that my grandfather had me do over the years I at least should be able to help one of his neighbors build a house for someone or, at a minimum, be his gopher. I didn't want to do it at all, but I also knew I had to begin doing something. My dad's neighbor came over to introduce himself and tell me where I'd be working and what he wanted me to do. The man's name was Samuel, and the house was going to be built about halfway between Richmond and Gwynn's Island in a little town named West Point. Everyone knows where West Point is because, if you go south towards the beach on Highway 64, you can always smell the paper mill. Cash and Ikey didn't have anything on that paper mill either. The next day, I drove to the site and the only thing that had been done to it was the foundation had been laid and that was about it. Other than that, the whole house needed to be finished.

I took a tent down with me because I wanted to stay down there as much as I could to give my parents a little break. They'd never ask for one, but I could see it in their eyes this was a lot on them too. I know when someone you love hurts, you hurt just as much, and I didn't want to hurt them anymore. My first week or so, I have to admit, I'd sloppily get through the day. I didn't necessarily half-ass anything, but I didn't outdo myself either. Samuel, the man I was supposed to be helping, was gone more than he was there so I was basically building the house all by myself anyway. I thought about just saying forget this crap and going back to my parents' house, but one day, when I guess Samuel could feel I was getting ready to give up, he told me who we were building the house for. He told me it was for the mother of a fallen soldier. My heart sunk when he explained that the survivors of that man's unit joined together to pay for a new house for their sergeant's mother as a final gift to him in remembrance.

He was their Chappy and for me from the second I heard about what I was doing this for it wasn't about me anymore in any way, problems or not. My crafty father knew what he was doing with his own lovingly-prescribed little project and, although I still couldn't say I was anywhere near being in a good place, I can say I worked as if my grandfather was right there beside me from that moment on. I made sure everything was more than perfect, and like my grandfather always did, I barely stopped during the three months it took to finish that cute little home. I got to the point where I didn't want Samuel to show up at all because I didn't think he would, or even could, put his heart into the job the way I needed to. I was building the house for that other sergeant's mother, but I was also building it for mine, for Chappy. Once I finished the house, at the home inspection, the man's mother burst into tears almost every time she'd enter another room. She couldn't believe how meticulously put together everything was. I then did something I can believe I'd do and I did something else that I didn't believe I'd ever do.

When she complimented my work, I gave credit to my grandfather, and, almost without thinking about it, I also gave credit to the military too. She was so happy with her new house that she invited me for dinner the first night she moved in. That was another time I didn't feel that I could refuse. As we sat and ate at the handmade dining table that I made specifically for her, I told her about how my grandfather taught me how to do all the things that she so lovingly appreciated, and since Gwynn's Island was so close, we spoke about it and West Point too. I was hesitant in asking about her son because I didn't know which chapter of that horror movie she was in. I didn't have to worry, though, because she told me all about him, and he seemed like a wonderful son. I already knew he was a wonderful sergeant because of what his family of brothers had done for him. I told her about Chappy, Jonas and Cash.

It's strange because I think I was helping her in other ways too just as she was for me. As the dinner ended, she hugged me, and I hugged her back. As I was leaving, my grandfather's definition of success popped in my head for some reason. It didn't just pop in my head—it was almost as if he had a megaphone screaming it from the great beyond and I thought I was hearing the message in his voice too. He said, "True success is how well you make the effort to care for others." With this house and for this lady and her overly familiar situation, I made every effort I knew how to. I knew she lost every bit as much as I did, if not more. She lost a child, and, if I thought life wasn't fair for me, I couldn't imagine what she had to be feeling. It's a cold and dark place that you're left with when you don't allow any light in. With this house for this particular lady and her heroic son, this was the first time since I'd been back home that I felt a little warmth from any sort of light myself.

After returning home, I thanked my father. I don't know how he did it or how he even knew what to do, but it helped so much. I guess, like I've been saying all along, that's what that kind of love does. I decided to help Samuel with another similar project for a while—which meant I built another house mostly by myself over the next two months. I'll never forget what happened, but I am getting a little better as each house goes up. I guess I'm letting more and more of that much-needed light in as well. It's kind of ironic that "work" is working for me the way it did for my grandfather I guess. It may have been for different reasons, but I am beginning to think he was right about the military; it does change you, and some of it might not be that bad after all. After I finished the next house, Samuel had another for me to work on at a place that was even closer to Gwynn's Island. It was in the little town of Mathews, VA. I was thinking that was getting a little too close for comfort for me. Although I was getting better, I still had this undercurrent of guilt living with me.

While I was in the hospital, they didn't even let me go to any of the funerals, and that alone haunts me because I never got a real chance to say goodbye to any of them. I'm also having these terrible nightmares at times, or should I say, nightmare, because it's always the same one over and over again. I don't have them every night, but the nights that I do are too many. I dream that I'm in a small courtroom that almost looks colonial for some reason. Everything from the pews where the onlookers sit to the juror's chairs and even the judge's bench are made from this deep, dark mahogany wood. They all have these intricate carvings of flowers throughout the wooden areas. They almost look like those damn lilies, I thought. All of the furniture's seating is covered with this regal yet aged burgundy leather and it has those gold beads pinning it down. The thing about it is, even though the courtroom is so clearly seen in these unwanted dreams, everybody who is in attendance is blurry for some reason.

I'm unable to see anything but these fuzzy outlines of who I think are many of the people that I've cared about in my life. The largest and least visible is the outline of the judge. Towards the end of the dream, before I'm woken, I start to feel like whoever it is in the courtroom with me is starting to become more recognizable. It's almost like a haze being lifted, but before anyone ever becomes fully identifiable, a giant gavel slams down and I hear the word "GUILTY" scream out in this thunderous voice. That voice and hearing the word "GUILTY" being howled out at me always terrifies me to wake. I guess I should be grateful that my nightmares aren't full of blood and gore anymore, but these dreams really do get to me. I always wake up in a beaded sweat and short of breath. I feel that I'm guilty of so many things in life but I have to wonder what it is that my dreams feel that I'm so guilty about and who are those almost translucent people, especially that judge who seems to want to punish me so badly.

Even though I didn't want to, I did agree to build the house with Samuel in Mathews. I always used to love that place too. With the exception of the bridge, Mathews and Gwynn's Island kind of seemed like one place to me when I was younger anyway. They have some pretty neat places to go as well. My family often ate at a few of the little rustic restaurants in their town square. Most of the time it was at Richardson's Café. They were all wonderful places and, even though my grandfather worked almost all the time, the one thing he always demanded was for all of his family—the ones who were down with him on the island at the time—to eat dinner together. Whether it was at home with my grandmother's extremely scrumptious meals, or, if we were lucky enough to go out to one of those fabulous restaurants, on almost every day his wishes were accomplished.

He liked to eat whenever and whatever he could, but those times were special to him—heck, they were special to all of us. When I say that man would eat anything, I mean it too. I guess being from a rural farming town in North Carolina will do that to you. He ate chitterlings, pig feet, pig eyeballs—I mean, any nasty thing that came from a pig, he'd eat it. Unfortunately, he'd always make us kids, to include me, at least try a bite of whatever grotesque thing he was eating too. By the way, if you've ever had souse meat and you like it, then something is very wrong with you. Chitterlings is the same if you ask me. For some reason, his culinary interest once gave us the little project of, I guess you'd say, planting an oyster bed in one of the creeks on the campground. I knew that big man liked to eat, and he'd pretty much eat anything, but why he wanted to grow his own oysters when everyone knew there were so many places to go get those blobby delicacies all around the island was a mystery to me. I guess I'll never know, but once again, if it saved him a dollar then I guess I already knew what he, or should I say we were going to do.

As Ikey, me and my grandfather were planting the oysters, which by the way, looked more like just throwing old oyster shells back, and spreading them around underneath with this huge twenty-pound metal rake. But I can remember being distracted by thinking about all of the different kinds of food I wish I could just throw down and spread out and then sit back and watch multiply. I guess I should have been paying more attention to what I was doing instead of daydreaming, but while drooling at my wishfully edible imagination, I stepped on one of those oyster shells that I had just thrown down myself. It ripped a gash in my foot from my pinky toe all the way across the ball of my foot. Water multiplies the looks of how much something is actually bleeding, and before long, everything around me was that crimson blood-red color. My grandfather didn't waste any time or question me in any way this time. I think he thought I was hurt worse than I actually was. With one of those big powerful paws, he threw me up over his shoulder and took off towards the only doctor's office that was anywhere around, which was in Matthews.

When we got there, the nurse grabbed me from my grandfather and, thankfully, she let me hobble back to the room on my own instead of carrying me. I wasn't back there long, but after twelve stitches across the bottom of my foot, it appeared I was going to live that time after all. Other than being the first time of many in my life to get stitches, I'll never forget that day because as strange as it sounds, the doctor that treated me was named Dr. Stitches. I had to be thinking, *Damn, what the hell? Once again?* The other reason was, it was the first time in my life that I saw my grandfather shaken in any way. I think he thought that I was hurt a lot worse than I was and it obviously scared him more than I thought that big man could be scared. He didn't cry or even have a tear in his eye, he just had that fearful look on his face. I could swear I heard him whispering out prayers on the way to Dr. Stitches for the stitches too.

That still cracks me up, but what I thought I heard him saying over and over again was, "Not my little buddy, God, not my little buddy." Thankfully, everything worked out well for him that day and for me too. It worked out so well that he took me to Richardson's Café afterward. I guess it was a reward for not being terminally hurt but it could have also been a declaration of gratitude for an answered prayer. No matter what it was, I was the winner. Richardson's was another reason I'll never forget that day. That little restaurant was kind of a 50's throwback, similar to how Hank's BBQ was in Richmond. After we were seated, my grandfather told me I could have anything I wanted, and I knew Richardson's didn't sell souse meat, so I felt safe in ordering their homemade chocolate cake for the first time out of many to come in my life. I think this was what Ikey was talking about when he told us about grace because I was getting the gift of Richardson's cake and I didn't have to do anything but cut my foot on an oyster shell to get it.

To confirm my thinking, my grandfather even let me eat it before I ate any vegetables, or anything else for that matter. Other than Mrs. Anna's Doppelgangers, or whatever you call those delicious, sugary cinnamon biscuit treats, Richardson's twelve-layer chocolate cake is as good as anything I've ever put in my mouth. *Twelve layers of chocolate might even make a kid get stitches from Dr. Stitches more often,* I thought. As we both sat there eating that utterly delicious cake, I could remember thanking God for not only the cake, which I did, but also for my grandfather and then for the rest of my family, to include Claire, Jonas and Ikey among others. I believe that was the second time that I can remember doing such a thing. Being that close to the island again while working in Mathews is bringing more of the better memories back to my soul. Maybe, just maybe I'm the one who's starting to let a little more of that much-needed light in myself.

# MY HEART GULPED

I guess it was a cowardly thing to do, but I just felt that the place I once loved more than anywhere else—the island—deserved better than what I still thought I was at the time. That feeling was still there, even with the gentle rays of light that were starting to poke through more often. Claire tried to call me a few times, but I still wouldn't speak to her. I guess I was trying to do with her the same as I was with the island and everyone else on it, and that was just to leave all of it in my mind as a beautiful memory, regardless of how close I was currently working to it then. I did talk to Ikey every now and then, but I never told him where I was. I'm still not the same person I once was, even with my current perceived improvements. What I had planned to do in staying away from the island changed about midway through the house project in Mathews. Like so many other things in my life, when life has a plan for you, it changes yours. However, that decision changed this time with one phone call from Mrs. Anna.

She told me this time it was Ikey's turn to go. By then, I expected Ikey to be almost two hundred years old, but seriously, I knew he was way up there, and, although I didn't want to think about it, I figured he would have passed away a long time ago. The guilt that I had for not spending enough time with my grandparents towards the end of their lives slammed back in my heart, but this time it was for Ikey, my lifelong royal guardsman. This time it may have even been a little worse because I was cowardly avoiding him over the past seven or eight months since I'd been home. I knew Jonas was Mrs. Anna's nephew—and Ikey's too after they got married—and even though I couldn't do anything to stop what happened to him, I knew I didn't help him either. After talking to Mrs. Anna for a while, she told me how sick Ikey was and that she didn't think he had much time left. She also said he kept asking for me, so she felt she had to make the call to see if I'd come. Once again, this was too big for me to ignore, especially after she put me on the phone with him for a few minutes.

He sounded bad. I couldn't make out most of what he said, but I do know he told me that he was going to be with the Lady in the Bay soon so I had better come see him as soon as I could. Then he let out a pitiful chuckle afterward. There was no way I could refuse what I knew had to be one of his final requests, so I agreed to go see him the next day. He still didn't know that I was only about fifteen minutes away in Mathews working. Before I hung up, he put Mrs. Anna back on the phone and she stressed the importance of me seeing him as quickly as I could. He seemed to have already outlived almost everyone else I knew, or longer than any normal person's life expectancy, but Ikey was never normal. If anyone could make me do what I didn't want to do, it was Ikey, and as he wished, that night I went to the Island and stayed in my grandparents' last house to get ready to see him the next day. My aunt and uncle took the place over after my grandparents died.

My grandparents would be so proud of how much work they put into the place—the things they didn't have time to do. My aunt and uncle put in a stone seawall and a new pier. I bet my uncle had the proper equipment for that little project too, and I doubt that he had to use that stupid electric pump that we did. They made the house look like a museum itself. I proudly knew it was their way of paying homage to some pretty special people in their lives as well. I know I owed being there to them to a degree and I know I owed Ikey at least one last visit as a final thank-you for all the beautiful things he did for all of us over the years also. Unlike with their nephew, or Cash and Chappy, this time I'd at least get to say goodbye in person. Once I made that short drive from Mathews to the island, I drove around to every landmark that I so lovingly remembered from my past. I saw Scrooch's store, the little post office in the middle of the island. I also drove past the seafood shops and the Hole in the Wall restaurant. I even forced myself to drive by the campground and Claire's parents' house.

If the what-ifs didn't consume me before, they definitely were at that point, but I just had to get them out of my mind. As I arrived at my grandparents' house, I went inside and saw my grandfather's old leather chair almost immediately after entering. My aunt probably kept it for the same reasons I would have. I kind of giggled as I saw a tobacco stain on the right arm of that puffy brown leather chair. I'm sure that stain, at one time or another, probably caused my grandmother to say, "That damn tobacco" too. I undeservedly sat in that big man's chair all night and the only thing that was completely out of my mind was sleep. This place and these people will always mean so much to me—that goes for my family who are blood-related and those who aren't as well. Somewhere in my own story I got lost and I really still don't know how to find my way back then either.

As I looked out of the bay window from my grandfather's chair, I saw the stars that Claire and I used to wish upon once again, but this time they seemed even closer because really they were on that little island. I also saw one of my grandmother's decorative sand dollars perched on a shelf on the back wall. I figured, as much as I needed it, there couldn't be much harm in going over and taking a look to see how much of what Ikey told us about them was actually true. I first remembered he said there were supposed to be five slashes on the outside, and there were. He also said there was a stamp of a star on one side and those damn bring-your-sweetheart flowers imprinted on the other. When I flipped it on each side, I saw that he was right about that too. Ikey then said, on the inside of each and every sand dollar there were five white doves. To him, they were the doves of love, forgiveness, courage, empathy and grace. I can remember that like it was yesterday. I also remember him telling Claire and I that the dove of love would always lead the other virtues, even if we couldn't see it or feel it at times.

I became a little angry thinking back about his description of the big dove because so many of the people that I loved just weren't here anymore and, evidentially, soon he wouldn't be either. I got so frustrated that I cracked that sand dollar open in my hand standing next to my grandfather's old leather chair. I wasn't mad or upset with Ikey at all, I think I was, as ridiculous at it sounds, mad at that dove hidden inside that Ikey spoke about. As I looked down at the mess I made from busting that thing open, I laughed because I saw them for myself. I saw the five white doves that Ikey told us would be there. I thought to myself, *I guess he was right again, that old buzzard*. As I sat there thinking about Ikey, my childhood, and even my adult life thus far, I thought about how Ikey fulfilled the twelve lessons from a sand dollar as much as anyone ever has in my opinion. I just hoped his dove of forgiveness would still be well enough to be able to express that virtue to me for not seeing him since I'd been back.

After a while, a smile came over my face thinking about what I knew of his life. No matter if it was a fake birthday party, toxic bug killer, an embarrassing gas issue, heatstroke, tobacco juice baths or pink culottes, he always made the most out of everything—well, maybe not "that damn tobacco," but with the other things, practically always. He worked—and he worked a lot—but work wasn't his life, people were, and he let them know it too. He always let me know it as well and I felt his words throughout my life. *What a great man and what a great life*, I thought. Even with his story about The Lady in the Bay and all of its embellishments, he was always trying to give us hope in the seemingly impossible and a sense of adventure in life. *What a tremendously loving way to be*, I proudly thought. I sat back down in my grandfather's chair for the rest of the night at that point. I still had all of those pieces of the sand dollar clinched in my hand. I guess, now that they've been somewhat proven to be true, I didn't want to let them go.

As I looked down at the mess I made one last time before I'd at least try to get a little sleep, I noticed that the sand dollar was star side up. I thought to myself, *maybe I have finally made it home*. The next morning heading to see Ikey I knew I'd have to drive by Claire's parent's house again. I didn't stop, although, even though I can't explain it, I could feel that she was there. I guess that connectedness takes quite a while to rub off and I hadn't quite reached that point yet, even though I was doing everything in my power to do so and now have for a long time. *That was then and this is now*, were the thoughts I was trying to stress in my mind. Besides, I'm here now to watch another wonderful friend of mine die, I guess. I deliberately took my time getting to Ikey and Mrs. Anna's. I'm pretty sure it was because I wasn't looking forward to seeing him in the way I figured he was going to be after hearing his voice in such a diminished state over the phone.

I made it there, though, and as I was walking up to the camper that he and Mrs. Anna still lived in at campsite seven, I remembered the first time we met Mrs. Anna. Ikey was so excited and drenched, not only from being in a suit in one-hundred-degree weather, but also I think because, somewhere in that old man's ability to see or at least direct the future, he knew that she'd be someone special in his life from that point on. As I knocked on the door, all I heard on the other end was silence. That was rare for Ikey, but those thoughts were from my past memories, so I don't guess it's like that anymore. I knocked on the door for about four or five times before someone answered. When they did, I didn't know who it was that was letting me in either. It was one of those times where I thought I knew who the lady was, but I wasn't sure, and neither Mrs. Anna nor Ikey were anywhere around to tell me. Strangely enough, the lady—who had to be around my mother's age or maybe just a little older—hugged me as I was coming in, and she directed me to sit down on the couch once I got inside.

At this point, I was thinking, *oh no, I was too late, and let another very special friend down before saying goodbye,* but that wasn't the case. The lady told me that Ikey was at the doctor's today, but he wanted me to come back tomorrow when they'd be back. She told me he asked me to do him a favor. I didn't know what else to say, but if Ikey needed one last favor from me, I'd do just about anything for my old friend, so I said, "Of course." The lady told me that the week before he got sick, he left his fishing pole at the tip of the island and he asked her to see if I could go get it for him. Everyone knows that the tip of the island is not only the best place to bury treasure at it's also the best place to fish from, so that seemed like an easy last request. Besides, now that I didn't have anything else to do, I might just use his rod and reel to do a little fishing or skate hunting myself. I remembered that you could get stranded with the tide if you weren't careful over there, and I also remembered that's exactly what happened when Claire, Jonas and I weren't careful.

So, not trusting myself to know any better, I asked the lady if she knew when the tide would be low enough to fulfill Ikey's last request safely. She was confident in her answer as she said, "4:00. Yep, I believe you should go at 4:00 and everything will work out fine." I was kind of shocked at her rapid and vast tidal knowledge that she just seemed to be able spurt out on a whim, but I thanked her and waited until 4:00 to go, especially since she seemed so positive that was the absolute best time to go. The tip of the island is only about a half-mile walk from Ikey's and Mrs. Anna's trailer, so I planned to park there and walk over when the time came. Since I had a little time to waste, I drove back to Scrooch's little country store. I didn't need anything, I just wanted to go to where my grandfather and I first met our very special friend. As I pulled up, almost nothing had changed. It was just as I remembered, with one very big exception. There was no cigar store Indian anywhere to be found.

As I got out of the car to go inside, I laughed a little when I got to the spot where I accidentally brushed against Ikey on the way in so many years ago. Little did I know then what that man would do for my family over the years. Once inside, I don't know why I picked up a pouch of tobacco—one that I'd never chew—but I did and began to take it to the register. I guess even little material things such as tobacco help with the pain every now and then. When I got to the register, even more pronounced than before, I could swear I heard my grandfather's voice. It was sounding off in my head if from nowhere else. When we went to Scrooch's when I was little, he was always rushing me out of the candy aisle. He'd often tell me that I didn't need whatever it was I wanted, which was usually a candy bar. However, this time, as confusing as it was, I felt like he or some mental illness of mine was telling me to go back and get the star bar.

He never got the names of any of my treats right, which I think I also inherited from him, but my mind, or someone from somewhere, was telling me to go get that Milky Way bar I was always trying to get him to buy me when I was younger. Again, I was just like him—I liked to eat—especially Milky Way bars, so who was I not to listen to whatever it was that was broadcasting those directions about treats between my ears for some unknown reason? As I walked back following my ethereal guidance, I saw a big black bucket with a bunch of flowers in it. I don't know why, but I grabbed two bunches of lilies and took them to the register as well. I guess I was really trying to cover up feelings with stuff, and for the time being, it was working a little. When I got back to Ikey's and Mrs. Anna's, I knocked on the door again just in case they may have gotten back from the doctor's office, but no one answered, not even the lady from before. I guess thinking about anybody going to a doctor in Mathews made me chuckle a little because it reminded me of Dr. Stitches giving me stitches, so I giggled a little that time too.

To get to the tip of the island, I knew I had to go by the beach that Claire and I spent so much time on in our youth. It was also Ikey's favorite place to tell his tales, so, in order for me to keep my feelings confined where I wanted them, I rushed past that beautiful little beach as fast as I could. Regardless of how quickly I was walking, I still swear I saw swirls in the water. That lady at Ikey's and Mrs. Anna's camper must have known what she was talking about because the passover to get across the inlet barely had any water in it at all, and I crossed over like there was nothing to it. As I was walking up to where the actual tip of the island was, there was somebody already there. I didn't recognize this person at first, and after I found out who it was, I didn't want to deal with any mess out of them at that time either. It was Tommy, that guy from the post office who hated us come-heres so much in my past.

I was cordial when I asked him if he knew where Ikey's fishing rod might be, but after he told me that he had it and he was using it, I think my mindset was starting to change a bit. I didn't want any crap out of this guy, I just wanted to get Ikey's fishing rod and leave, but he wouldn't let me. I tried to calm myself down at least outwardly because this guy didn't realize that I may still have some of those pretty serious monsters in me. What happened next made me feel like more of an ass than I already thought I was. As I clearly and outwardly began to get upset with him, he started to cry. I know I cried to my parents when I first saw them in the hospital; I know if I was honest, I still cried myself to sleep at times, but there's an unwritten guy rule that you just don't cry to another dude who you barely know, especially one that you've hated for as long as he's hated me for simply not being from the same place he was. After I kind of backed off, he asked me to sit down so we could talk. I still didn't really want to talk to this guy, I just wanted to get Ikey's fishing rod and leave, but I obliged him instead. That guy then pulled out a grocery bag from the other side of a big piece of driftwood near where he was fishing and slid it over to me.

His tears didn't lessen any after he told me that he didn't do his job as the island's postman as he should have. He said inside that bag were all the letters that Claire sent me while I was gone and he did the same with the ones I wrote her too. I don't know if it was guilt or if Ikey found out about what happened and wanted him to make things right—as right as he could make it at that point anyway. After he told me about the letters in front of me he also told me he dropped Claire's bag of letters off to her the day before. I sat there a few minutes not knowing how to feel. There was nothing I could do to the guy that he wasn't already doing to himself, so I did the only thing I knew to do and forgave him. I felt like I was forgiving him with a frog in my mouth and this didn't mean that we'd be going fishing or out to lunch together anytime soon in the future, but what could I do?

After a few minutes of silence, I asked him again for Ikey's fishing rod and, this time, he gave it up easily. I also asked him if I could have some time alone to think, so he obliged me this time and left. Hopefully he left to actually deliver the mail this time but at least he left me alone to think. Not that long ago it felt like I was a million miles from nowhere, and, little by little, I have been at least getting closer to somewhere. To be completely honest, I don't know if this news from Tommy puts me closer to where I needed to be or not. I sat in almost the exact same spot that we buried that old, red toolbox so many years ago for at least a solid hour wondering where I go from here. Like with most things in my life, it really wasn't ever my decision to make alone though. After what I thought was an hour, but may have been a few of sitting there, talking to myself and thinking about so many things, especially Claire, I realized the tide was almost all of the way in and I was trapped out there for quite a while again.

As I sat there getting ready to dig in for what I knew was going to be another 4 to 6 hours or more, I remembered putting that Milky Way—or "star bar," as my subliminal grandfather called it—in my backpack. I never let my treats simmer that long, and I couldn't believe I did it that time either. I was getting hungry with all this emotional stuff going on, so I was glad I did. When I opened my backpack, I saw the flowers and the chewing tobacco that I also bought inside. I didn't really have a plan for either of them because I wasn't going to give either one of them away—or chew either one of them either for that matter. I did take them out of my backpack and lay them down on the sand beside me. I laid them close to where the bag of letters and the confusion Tommy left me with were. For a split second I thought about trying to take a chew as my grandfather did so many times, but this time, it was almost as if I heard my grandmother's voice saying, "You better leave that damn tobacco alone," so I put it down pretty quickly. Alive or not, she was pretty tough in her own right and I knew it.

As I laid the flowers on the sand, what I feared and what I hoped for, even longed for, happened all at once. I heard that sweet-sweet voice that I missed so much ask me if those flowers I had just taken out were for her. It was Claire, and I knew it without a shadow of a doubt. I couldn't fully look up though. I couldn't even take a peek because, if I did, I knew those eyes would have sank me once again and I'd be done just like the first time I ever saw her. She came over and sat next me and next to all the things that I had sprawled out on the beach, to include that newly discovered grocery bag of letters that just happened to all be from her. I must have been like a little shy kid ignoring someone he had a crush on. This was another time like when I was a kid and couldn't show my true joy, even though the person who made me the most joyous was sitting there right next to me once again. I didn't have a bedroom door to lock myself behind this time though. We were going to be stuck there for hours together.

She didn't say a lot at first and I didn't say anything because I wasn't at the point where I knew what to think yet. She just sat beside me with her head on my shoulder as we both watched the tide come in. I don't know when I started talking, but, for some reason, I felt that I had to defend myself. I started talking about the letters, but Claire stopped me. She said, "I know, but that was then, and this is now." I smiled because I knew she was right. There was no way to go back and change what happened. She was so right that, if she had a pen and paper, she would have probably checked and hearted her rightness too—smart aleck. Little by little, as we began to talk, the more recent past seemed like a distant memory. We were there together now and there was nothing else in the world around us, except for, as Ikey would say, Mawi Hewa and Ekiwa Hewa—right heart and left heart.

I have to give myself a little credit this time because I didn't stutter even one word, but I did feel like I might at times. Claire told me that Tommy stopped by her parents' house on the way out and let her know that I was there. He also apologized a few more times to her. It never ends well for the person who hates someone so much just because they're different or from somewhere else. Claire and I talked about everything, and I mean everything, for the hours that we were trapped out there and even throughout the night after we could have left. We talked for so long that it felt like we knew each other from the beginning of time once again—our limited time on earth anyway. I asked her about not coming to the airport and she told me she was there. She just couldn't make it inside. She said she stayed outside crying almost all night in the parking lot, especially after seeing my jet take off and then go out of sight. We talked about Jonas and how if there was ever a shooting star to make it home, it was him. She told me his mother, a lady she called Ruby, had been staying with Ikey and Mrs. Anna because she had plans to move down to the island or somewhere close.

Once again I thought I may know something at this point, but I still couldn't quite put my finger on it, so I moved on and started reminiscing about Ikey a little. I wanted to know what she knew about his situation, but I guess it was just too hard for her because she never really said anything back about our old, tanned buddy. We even talked about the Lady in the Bay and all of our adventures that often set us off in every direction after hearing such possibilities. It was a beautiful time that we spent together in our childhood and it was that time on the tip of the island too. The one thing that she did say about Ikey was that he'd been busy since I left. Almost all of the kids, to include the come-here's like I was, knew our story about the Lady in the Bay, and almost all of them had found their own necklace made from seashells, sand dollars and arrowheads just like ours. She said he had the whole island and half of Mathews involved in getting these kids to believe they could achieve the seemingly impossible.

All they had to do, she said, was believe she exists, keep his secret and wholeheartedly seek her out just like we did. I laughed thinking back at all that we did to seek our Lady in the Bay out, but Claire assured me that the kids now are doing even more and it was a beautiful sight. Once the time came to where we felt it was time to go, she was almost rushing me to follow her out. This time with Claire on the beach was almost overwhelming once again. It was almost like I never left for both of us. I've always known how I felt about her and I also knew that would never change, no matter what I ever tried to tell myself, but there was no way I could have ever expected the twists and turns that life presented that day. Before we crossed back over, I leaned down and grabbed my backpack, the tobacco, and my star bar that I still hadn't had a chance to eat. I also grabbed those two bunches of lilies. I told Claire that I could only give her one just in case Ikey had forgotten to give his sweetheart some for a while.

M. A. COLE

# TRUE TREASURE

**B**efore we left the tip of the island, for the first time in a very long time, I looked up at what I knew about God now and thanked him. Meeting that little blonde girl changed my life and I had a feeling that re-meeting this blonde young woman will too. I know, as I have for a long time, that there are some people who come into your life who just seem to fit, no matter what age you are, or what you've ever been through, you just know they are, as unexplainable as it may be, a predestined gift from above. Claire was always that for me and I know I was always that for her too. As we crossed the inlet, our first plans together as whatever we were now was to go to see Ikey. He'd be so happy for us, and since it was Claire's idea and most likely would have been checked and hearted if she had any paper once again, I knew that's what we were going to do. For me at least, our walk started a little on the somber side because I knew what we'd probably see when we got to Ikey's and, especially now, I just wasn't ready to lose him too.

As we walked, the closer we got to that little beach that was so special to our childhood—and the one we had to walk past to get to Ikey and Mrs. Anna's. With every step closer, I could swear I was hearing a noise blowing out from the past. Now, earlier that day, I also thought I heard my grandfather telling me to get a candy bar and my grandmother saying, "Put the damn tobacco down," so I didn't put too much stock in my hearing at this time, but, with every step this time, I knew I was hearing something, and it wasn't just something, it was something I knew wasn't just in my mind. I halfway rationalized that there may be a puffy-haired man performing on the beach. Instead, when we got all the way there, it wasn't Elvis playing, it wasn't Santa Claus either—it was our very own sickly-tanned man, the Lady in the Bay "himself." Remember I'm not saying that old, tan man would lie to get something he wanted, but he did, and he did it more than once too, and he was doing it right then to me.

Ikey may have been old, but he looked wonderful, and happy too, as he was playing that harmonica as well as he ever did. Once he saw Claire and me, he stopped playing and came over to hug us, and, of course, that old codger winked at me. He told us that they were having Gwynn's Island's own Lady in the Bay day and being that he was going to name me as the grand marshal, he had to make sure that I came down. Now, I knew I was old enough to say, "Damn, What the hell man", so I did. Ikey laughed and pulled me onto a makeshift stage—the one my old fake sick friend was playing from earlier. There must have been everyone from the island and most of Mathews County there too. Looking around, I saw the high school band and members of the coast guard in attendance as well. I'd never been the grand marshal of anything before and, although I was appreciative, I was actually trying to sneak off of the stage without anyone noticing.

It didn't work though because Conway and that same damn three-legged dog, Pogo, were standing guard at the end of the steps. Conway was cussing and smacking his lips while sneaking a sip of his favorite beer in when he could, and that damn dog was looking at my leg a little too flirtatiously for my taste just like old times. I thought to myself, *how in the hell is that dog still alive,* but that thought was something else I'd never admit to. After Ikey held his hands in the air to quiet the large crowd, he brought Claire, Mrs. Anna and the lady who let me in their camper on stage with us. Somehow my parents made the ride down from Richmond too and snuck in the crowd of people without me knowing it until Ikey brought them on stage as well. Mrs. Anna leaned over to me before Ikey started speaking and told me that it was her German Fran Brothchens, those sugary cinnamon biscuit treats, that was keeping Ikey so young, and then she winked at me just like he would. *What is it with these old people and winking at me,* I thought.

I smiled at her in response because, hey, even if she did help Ikey with his fabricated illness tale to evidentially get me down there at a specific time for a specific reason—which worked by the way—I already knew she was family too. Ikey told the crowd that he selected a few people to talk about why I'd be worthy of such a prize as being grand marshal at the Lady in the Bay day parade. This is sounding more and more familiar to me, kind of like when Ikey told us we had to include those letters about each other in that old, red toolbox treasure chest, but good or bad, this time at least I'd get to hear what people thought I guess. Now more than ever I knew that I'd be giving Ikey his Indian name and it would definitely be Chief Fulla Bulla, but how much more thankful could I be that his name would be so fitting for my benefit. This time back with everyone here on the island was absolutely wonderful and strange with all this stuff going on too, but with Ikey, the stranger things seemed to be, the more they'd somehow end up helping someone who wouldn't have let it happen any other way.

That someone, in this case, was me. One of my favorite parts of the day was when they allowed me to speak about Jonas, and as I did, I told the crowd about how brave he was and how much he loved the island. Afterwards, I was so humbled as my loved ones began to speak about me. Ikey told a story about two braves who both earned an eagle feather and how one brave, through the love for the other, gave his away. He never mentioned our names, but I knew. I didn't know how he knew that story unless my parents told him, but he always knew everything anyway. Claire spoke next, and she spoke about forgiveness and how life rarely works out as we plan, however, with some things, as she pointed out, they may just end up even better than we could have ever imagined. My loved ones' words were hitting me in the heart kind of hard.

When my parents spoke, they told everyone how proud they were of how far I'd come and how much of that was because of the houses that I was working on for people who have experienced similar tragedies. When the crowd cheered, I thought I was going to cry worse than Tommy did, but my tears weren't from regret, they were from being so grateful that those I loved, loved me so much. Then, the most full circle thing that I've ever experienced occurred. Mrs. Anna walked up to speak, and when she did, she brought the lady that she'd been standing beside on stage with her. She was the one who let me in their camper the other day. Miss Anna introduced her to the crowd as not only her sister, Ruby, but also the person who I was currently building the house for in Mathews. I may have not fully connected the dots before, and in fairness, she never fully let me in on the secret either, but I knew now that this lady, Ruby, was Jonas' mother.

She hugged me and I hugged her back, and we cried—almost as bad as the first time I saw my parents in the hospital. The whole crowd was crying and clapping at that point. From there, I have no words to describe what I was feeling or what everybody experienced that day other than saying it just pure love everywhere. I don't want to try and explain it in any other way because no other words could do that time any more justice. After Ikey played his harmonica a while longer with the high school band, and after everyone ate and played games until they had their fill, my family and everyone who were up on the stage that day met at Ikey and Mrs. Anna's. It was a little cramped, but we didn't mind. Ruby, Jonas' mother, came over to me at the same couch she told me to sit down on the last time I was there. She told me that, even though we never met, she felt like she knew me through all of Jonas' letters and all he had told her about me. He evidentially felt the same way that I felt about him, and I couldn't think of a better person to hear it from. I was speechless from pride.

She knew I was feeling guilty and had been for a long time, but she did everything in her power to let me know she felt he was more than fine now. It's not that she didn't hurt or miss him greatly, but even in his short life, she stated how he was able to give so much of himself to others. She said she knew and learned with time that his death was his natural and blessed next move to an even better mansion with his father and with the divine father too. As Ruby got up to go help Mrs. Anna in the kitchen with what I'm sure was more of those sugary cinnamon biscuit treats, the others must have gotten to her too because she winked at me like they all would do. That wink made my heart smile and, although it may not be complete closure, it was another great blast of light that was being forced in, and there was nothing at all I could do to block it by using anything that I'd been through. This time at the island light had broken through so much for me. Before, I thought it was me who controlled how much light I allowed in, but on this day, it was my friends—no, my family—who so lovingly brought me fully back to life and all the way into an illumination. That's what that kind of love can do. I still can't believe that old, tanned bugger faked a terminal illness and had everyone in on it, to include Mrs. Anna, Claire, and even my parents just to get me back down to the island.

He's known where I've been and what I was doing the whole time I've been back. He just wanted wanted to give me time and of course wait for the perfect time for the right fabrication to pull off everything in a way that only he could. I then remembered that I had another bunch of lilies in my backpack for him to give to Mrs. Anna. When I gave them to him, he smiled and thanked me, but he also said that he had one more surprise for Claire and me. Of course, that was only after he asked me where his fishing rod was. Ikey told Claire and me to go to our old Fort Fishing Shack, the one that my grandmother would have definitely compared to a pig with lipstick. When we got there, I soon realized that little shack smelled worse than I remembered.

Across from the door, next to the sink where we cleaned so many fish in the past, and where we hearted so many of our future plans, there was our next surprise. It was that old, red toolbox treasure chest. Claire and I laughed at the thought of Ikey possibly being out at the tip of the island wading in the water with pink culottes on, or maybe even swimming around with a snorkel looking for it. Then we remembered those things would be nothing to a man who would do anything just to help those he loved believe they could achieve the impossible. I don't know how he got it back, and I don't I guess I ever will, but as Claire and I opened my grandfather's old toolbox, the one I pretty much stole years ago, all of what I consider as true treasures were still inside unharmed. We saw the necklace made of seashells, sand dollars and arrowheads, and we also saw all the letters that we wrote about each other, to include the ones that Ikey wrote about us.

Somehow they were still as pristine as the day we wrote them. The smell of that old shack didn't bother us anymore as Claire and I read every single word from each letter sitting on the floor of that little shack together. All the time that passed and everything that happened over the past few years didn't seem to matter anymore. This was especially true for me and Claire because, the one thing that became extremely clear to both of us again was, there are some people who come into your life who just seem to fit, no matter what age you are or what you've ever been through, you just know they are, as unexplainable as it may be, a gift from above. I know, as I have always known, that we were all that for each other, and whether here or there or anywhere, we always will be too. If all goes well and Claire and I get to the place where we do get married and have kids, I pray I can always remember all the stories that Ikey told us. I wonder if they'll ever figure out for themselves that the Lady in the Bay was actually a really-really old—some say, woolly mammoth or even nipple tooth—old, wrinkled, tan man.

Dear Friends,

Thank you for choosing our inspirational products! We'd love for you to visit our website at www.inkwillpublications.com to check out our full range of offerings. We hope our products will help uplift your spirits and inspire you on your journey. So, as my old buddy Ikey would say, "May the Lady in the Bay bless you on your way"!

Best regards,
M. A. Cole
Inkwill Publications

www.ingramcontent.com/pod-product-compliance
Lightning Source LLC
Chambersburg PA
CBHW072231190626
46809CB00017B/1696